*By the Rivers of Babylon*

RUTGERS PRESS *fiction*

*By the Rivers*

*f Babylon*

AND OTHER STORIES

*Jorge de Sena*

*Edited and with a Preface by Daphne Patai*

RUTGERS UNIVERSITY PRESS
*New Brunswick and London*

Original stories copyright © Mécia de Sena
Preface and English translations copyright © 1989 by Rutgers, The State
University
All rights reserved
Manufactured in the United States of America

Library of Congress Cataloging-in-Publication Data
Sena, Jorge de.
"By the rivers of Babylon", and other stories/Jorge de Sena; edited by Daphne Patai.
p. cm.
Translated from Portuguese.
ISBN 0-8135-1388-X
1. Sena, Jorge de—Translations, English. I. Patai, Daphne, 1943 – . II. Title.
PQ9261.S337A2 1989
869.3'42—dc19                                                  88-21100
                                                                    CIP

British Cataloging-in-Publication information available

# Contents

Editor's Preface                                    vii

The Story of the Duck-Fish                            1

Sea of Stones                                        19

The Corner Window                                    31

The Commemoration                                    63

The Russian Campaign                                 79

Kama and the Genie                                   87

A Night of Nativity                                 101

The Great Secret                                    117

A Very Brief Tale                                   123

Defense and Justification of
     a Former War Criminal                          127

By the Rivers of Babylon                            141

# Editor's Preface

*J*ORGE DE SENA (1919–1978) was his own best and most prolific commentator. "I myself am my country," he wrote in his long 1965 poem "In Crete, with the Minotaur" as he approached his second experience of exile, this time from Brazil to the United States:

> Born in Portugal, of Portuguese parents,
> and father of Brazilians in Brazil,
> I'll perhaps be North American once I'm there.
> I'll collect nationalities like shirts to be stripped off,
> used and discarded, with all the respect
> due clothing we wear and that has served us well.
> I myself am my country. The country
> of which I write is the language into which
>     by the accident of generations
> I was born. And the one with which I create and
>     by which I live is this
> rage I feel at the paltry humanity of this world
> when I can believe in no other, and would only want
>     another
> if it were this very one. But, if one day I should
>     forget everything,
> I'd hope to grow old
> sipping coffee in Crete

with the Minotaur,
beneath the gaze of shameless gods.[1]

Ever bristling at tiny Portugal's closed scholarly and artistic circles from which he, intellectually an autodidact, felt largely excluded, ever critical of the Salazar regime, as of all other forms of authoritarianism, Sena was nonetheless an intensely Portuguese writer. When I first knew him, at the University of Wisconsin in 1969–70 during my first year there as a graduate student and his last year there as a professor, he often used to say: "The tragedy of Portuguese literature is that it is written in Portuguese." But this was his language, and he explored it lovingly in a variety of genres which together constitute an extraordinarily rich and diverse body of work that, even before his death, established Sena as Portugal's preeminent contemporary man of letters.

Jorge de Sena was born in Lisbon on November 2, 1919, the only child of Maria da Luz Telles Grilo and Augusto Raposo de Sena. His father, originally from the Azores, was a commander in the Merchant Marine and Sena was from early childhood destined for the Navy. At the age of seventeen, Sena entered the Naval Academy in Lisbon, but the inhospitable political climate brought his naval career to a close in 1938. By this time Sena was already writing poetry, an activity begun in 1936 upon—so he tells us—hearing Debussy's "Cathédrale Engloutie." Although throughout his life he considered himself first and foremost a poet, the years 1937 and 1938 also saw his early experiments with short fiction. In fact, from his very first publications in 1939 to the end of his life, Sena simultaneously cultivated poetry and prose. He wrote short stories, essays,

---

1. My translation. The original text and a slightly different translation by Frederick G. Williams are available in *The Poetry of Jorge de Sena: A Bilingual Selection,* ed. Frederick G. Williams (Santa Barbara: Mudborn Press, 1980), pp. 196–201.

poetry, literary history, immensely erudite volumes of literary analysis, drama, novel and novella, translations—and in each of these genres he produced substantial work: dozens of volumes published in his lifetime, and a stream of books still being brought out posthumously by Mécia de Sena, his wife and constant companion. In 1942, *Perseguição*, Sena's first published volume of poetry, appeared. This was to be followed by more than a dozen additional volumes before his death. Sena's first piece of literary criticism was also published in 1942 and was succeeded, in his lifetime, by more than twenty volumes of critical essays and literary analysis. In 1944 he began to publish translations. Fluent in English at a time when most educated Portuguese were oriented entirely toward French culture, Sena translated Edgar Allan Poe, Graham Greene, Ernest Hemingway, Evelyn Waugh, William Faulkner, and André Malraux, among other writers of fiction, as well as a number of dramatists and poets, most notably Eugene O'Neill, Bertolt Brecht, C. P. Cavafy, and Emily Dickinson (one of Sena's favorite poets).

Sena's intellectual range was enormous. I clearly recall his encyclopedic lectures when I was his student. Deploring the "two cultures" debate, he saw the sciences and the humanities as complementary. He was a humanist in a sense rarely used today, a man intensely concerned with the human condition, possessed of wide and deep learning, and passionately engaged with the aesthetic and political dimensions of language.

In 1938, after his brief naval career, he returned to school—not to study literature, but rather to qualify in civil engineering. By the time he graduated from the University of Oporto in 1944, however, he was already writing about Fernando Pessoa, Portugal's brilliant and multifaceted twentieth-century poet (who wrote in English as well as in Portuguese). Following a one-year stint of military service in 1945, Sena went to work as a bridge engineer, principally with Portugal's

National Highway Commission, a career he continued until he
changed countries and professions in 1959. In that year, feeling
himself to be in a precarious position in Portugal because of his
opposition to Salazar, Sena took advantage of an invitation to
participate in the Fourth International Conference on Luso-
Brazilian Studies, held in Brazil at the University of Bahia, and
voluntarily went into exile. His family joined him three months
later, leaving Salazar's Portugal for still-democratic Brazil. In an
essay written two years before his death, Sena stated that he was
never part of any political or literary group and had friends of all
persuasions, with the exception only of committed fascists.
Until his exile from Portugal, he tells us, he was involved more
or less clandestinely in anti-Salazarist politics. Once in Brazil,
he openly opposed the Salazar regime.[2] Throughout this period,
he taught theory of literature and Portuguese literature at the
Assis and Araraquara branches of the University of São Paulo
and continued his diverse literary endeavors, which, in addition
to the genres noted above, included music, theater, and film
criticism.

Sena became a Brazilian citizen in 1963. He did not give
up this citizenship during his second exile, which began in
1965, the year after the military came to power in Brazil. He
then went to the United States—initially as a visiting professor
at the University of Wisconsin in Madison. Shortly before his
death, when asked why, after thirteen years in the United
States, he had still not become an American citizen, he replied
that neither Brazilians nor Portuguese liked his Brazilian citizenship, both for the same reason: that he was born Portuguese.
"So just to irritate both," he said, he had retained it.[3]

I met Jorge de Sena in September 1969, at the beginning

2. "O Poeta e o Crítico na mesma Pessoa—Um Depoimento sobre Al-
gumas Décadas de Experiência Pessoal," in Jorge de Sena, *Dialécticas Teóricas da
Literatura* (Lisboa: Edições 70, 1977), p. 241.
    3. "O Poeta e o Crítico," p. 241.

of his last complete year at the University of Wisconsin. Here was a professor who, while ostensibly teaching us the literature of a small European country, took the entire world as his arena. Always outspoken, he did not suffer fools easily. Often irascible, he was also generous. And, most of all, he was eager to share with his students his vast culture and enthusiasm for intellectual work. In a time still dominated by formalist criticism, he was preeminently a committed critic and writer, using all available tools but bringing to this use his passionate political and ethical commitments. He was later to write that he had always considered literature inevitably *engagé*, but under no obligation to carry out party guidelines.[4]

In the spring of 1970, when the United States invaded Cambodia, the University of Wisconsin was immobilized by a weeks-long strike. Sena supported the strike, though he complained bitterly that it made creative work virtually impossible. Meanwhile, he held classes in his home, a dilapidated house with fragments of ceiling hanging down into the living room where we sat, and room-high bookshelves occupying every available bit of space, along hallways, even in the kitchen. After the classes, he and Dona Mécia used to stand in the doorway of the house, waving good-bye to us as we walked down the street, a heartening portrait of unity and companionship. This is the image I still carry with me, for I never saw him again after that year.

Sena then moved to the University of California at Santa Barbara, where he served as chairman of both the Departments of Spanish and Portuguese, and of Comparative Literature. His immense productivity continued, not only his own poetry and fiction, but his lifetime dedication to Portugal's two master poets, each the subject of several of Sena's most important

4. Cited by Frederick G. Williams in his introduction to *The Poetry of Jorge de Sena: A Bilingual Selection*, p. 16.

volumes of literary criticism: the great sixteenth-century lyric and epic poet Luís de Camões (subject of the title story of this volume), and his twentieth-century compatriot Fernando Pessoa. During the 1970s, in the last decade of his life, Sena received numerous honors and awards, including, in 1977, the prestigious Etna-Taormina International Poetry Prize.

Jorge de Sena died in Santa Barbara on June 4, 1978. He was not yet sixty years old. That year, six books of his were published. Since then many more have appeared under the stewardship of Mécia de Sena.

In recent years Sena's poetry and fiction have been translated into many languages: French, German, Italian, Chinese, Catalan, Spanish, Bulgarian, Flemish, Greek, Hungarian, Yugoslav, Lithuanian, Rumanian, and Swedish. In the English language, however, Sena is thus far best known as a poet, for it is above all his poetry that has appeared in translation, starting with the 1966 publication of Jean R. Longland's anthology, *Selections from Contemporary Portuguese Poetry*, [5] and continuing with the appearance of several individual volumes.

The present book is the first sampling of Jorge de Sena's short fiction to be made available in English, and the translation problems it represents are formidable. Unlike the classical simplicity of much of Sena's poetry, his fiction typically utilizes a rich and copious style, with innumerable embedded clauses creating a web of unusual density. The overarching sense evoked by such a style is of a reality that is immensely complex and interwoven, one that the syntax of simple declarative sentences would destroy. The translators of these stories, and I myself as editor of the volume and also as translator, have attempted to respect Sena's style and to render its density and rhythms within the possibilities of the English language. Mécia de Sena, with

5. Jean R. Longland, ed., *Selections from Contemporary Portuguese Poetry* (Irvington-on-Hudson, N.Y.: Harvey House, 1966).

her own experienced translator's eye and deep knowledge of her husband's work, suggested corrections and revisions to all the translations.

The first five stories in this volume originally appeared in Sena's 1960 collection *Andanças do Demónio* [Wanderings of the Devil]. In his preface to that volume Sena describes these stories as varied, containing a bit of everything, unified only in that all reveal "demoniacal perambulations," but declines to identify in them "the undesired traveller."[6] Explaining his conception of the short story, Sena states that, unlike the novella, it is a momentary narrative, a suspension in time; and, unlike the novel, it is less an animated meditation on life than a dreamy contemplation of it.

The last six stories translated here appeared in the 1966 volume *Novas Andanças do Demónio* [Further Wanderings of the Devil]. Again Sena added what he called "one of my inevitable prefaces," written in 1964, this time to excoriate the complete decadence, servility, and totalitarianism of the Portuguese critical establishment and its support of a purely conventional realism. Yet Sena's larger aim in writing prefaces was, he stated, to explain his work to the public, not to the critics, and he therefore proceeds to distinguish these new wanderings of the devil from the earlier volume: a fantastic realism or imaginary historicism predominates in the new stories, with a corresponding decrease in autobiographical stories or those dealing with current or conventional reality. "Realism," in Sena's conception, depends not at all on a dogged fidelity to a contemporary setting. On the contrary, he writes, traditional realism is more likely to be a spurious form of immobilizing reality, which, by its essence, is in process of becoming. A complete or partial

6. The following comments draw on Sena's own prefaces and notes to the stories, in *Antigas e Novas Andanças do Demónio* (Lisboa: Edições 70, 1978), pp. 247–267.

fantasy, Sena writes, can far better convey a realistic intensity, whereas traditional realism, when not subjective—when not, that is, arising from a revolt of our personal memories—is no longer valid. Our world is so fragmented, the unity of character imposed by writers on their fictional creations so suspect, that we would do better, Sena says, to be objective with fantasy and subjective with reality.

Discussing his right to utilize an elegant and discrete "fin-de-siècle" style to deal with the distant historical figures of Tiberius and St. Paul (see "A Night of Nativity"), Sena defines a personal style as "an attitude that one assumes, an orientation that one chooses, an individual obliqueness in dealing with things and people, a structure that one builds out of them and out of language." A writer, in this conception, has as many "styles" as the things of which he or she speaks.

Sena's two volumes of stories were later combined and, with his prefaces and notes, published in 1978 as *Antigas e Novas Andanças do Demónio* [Old and New Wanderings of the Devil]. From this volume I selected eleven stories, which appear in the present book in a slightly altered sequence. I also enlisted the help of five other translators, all former students or colleagues of Jorge de Sena and currently professors of Portuguese in the United States.

The stories represent two decades of work, and some of them, as the dates Sena placed at the end of each text indicate, were finished or revised many years after they were begun. To stories focusing on historical figures (e.g., "Sea of Stones," about the Venerable Bede, and especially the title story, about Luís de Camões—himself for a time an involuntary exile, as the story recounts—and the composition of one of his most famous poems), Sena appended long bio-bibliographical notes. Concerning "By the Rivers of Babylon," Mécia de Sena has written:

> It is far more autobiographical than people realize. To
> begin with, Camões is without doubt the great domi-

nating figure in my husband's life and work. I have concluded that a sonnet sequence (for example) that he wrote soon after receiving the proofs of one of his books on Camões, not only corresponds in number of verses to the poem studied in this book, but the analysis of the poet/human being/thinker that the book sets out at precisely this point is a self-analysis. And with this story he goes further still. In an intermittent diary, my husband unfolds the events of a particular day and, at the end, says: "And I wrote, until four o'clock in the morning, a story I was not anticipating: 'By the Rivers. . . .'" If one recalls that the story ends with the words "And he wrote on into the night . . ." it is apparent that he was speaking of himself, actually transposing the immediate situation. In addition, the model for that mother is his own mother, who also appears, to biting effect, in "The Corner Window."[7]

Of the stories translated here, "The Corner Window" is perhaps the most complex syntactically. Especially in its opening pages, one encounters Sena's tendency to confront his readers with a dense and defiant prose, resistant to easy comprehension, as if proclaiming—as other writers have done—"Do not understand me too quickly!"

Sena's notes on the stories provide us with further information as to his sources and intents. These comments are of particular interest for an understanding of Sena's own view of his work, but they are not indispensable, for the stories, though sometimes difficult, are accessible. The range of themes and treatments in these stories is great, but almost all are, in one way or another, character studies, and the loving accumulation of detail finally conveys to the reader images of startling intensity and depth. Some of the stories are satirical in intent, though

7. Letter from Mécia de Sena to DP, dated 7 May 1987. My translation.

a considerable distance separates the gentle humor of "Kama and the Genie" (1964), with its theme of the transmigration of souls, from the biting portrayal in "The Commemoration" (1946) of Portugal's colonial administrators ever living in the shadow of their African reminiscences. Sena, whose maternal grandparents had emigrated to Angola in the nineteenth century, tells us that this story, originally published in a journal in 1947, was one of the first literary denunciations of the Portuguese colonial adventure, as well as a satire on the fad for commemorations endemic to Salazar's "Estado Novo."

The scathing exposé of the Nazi mentality in "Defense and Justification of a Former War Criminal," written in 1961, reveals Sena's lifelong hatred of fascism in all its forms, and his particular disdain for the intellectual pretensions of Nazism. Stories such as "The Great Secret," "A Night of Nativity," and "Sea of Stones," reveal his fascination for things related to saintliness and early Christianity. Sena's attraction to surrealism is apparent in "The Russian Campaign," conceived in 1946, revised in 1960, which he described, shortly before his death, as one of the final pieces of his immense multivolume novel *Monte Cativo* (of which only the first book, *Sinais de Fogo,* published in 1979, was completed). Though differing in the worlds they evoke, many of the stories—for example, "The Story of the Duck-Fish" (1959) and "The Corner Window" (1950–1960)— explore the theme of isolation and relation. "The Duck-Fish" began life when Sena's young children, feeling excluded from his writing, requested that he compose a story for them. What emerged, however, was far from the children's tale Sena sat down to write. And several of the stories deal with the process of composition itself. "A Very Brief Tale" (1961) does so in a ludic mode, "By the Rivers of Babylon" (1964) in a somber one. But even this title story, for all its sobriety and painful exploration, has its small comic moments.

Twice exiled, forever estranged—in but never of whatever

country he inhabited—Jorge de Sena was quick to see the touches of absurdity in the most painful or serious situation, quick to probe the tender core of human fragility hiding in the crassest incident. His stories, scathing and ardent, fantastic and mundane, move delicately from the world to the word—and back again.

Daphne Patai
*Bloomington, Indiana*
*July 1988*

*By the Rivers of Babylon*

# The Story of the Duck-Fish

And they began to eat the meat that
the other man had brought and they
died of the poison that was in it.

Orto do Esposo

*T*HERE was once a man who lived in a very small cabin
on the seashore, somewhere along the coast of Africa, India, or
Brazil, where the heat is so great that the sea looks like blue
glass and the forests grow so high that they press down, down,
and even come to the foot of the water. In such a setting the poor
man had hardly any place to put up his cabin. Between the
waves and the trees there was only a tiny little narrow strip of
sand, good for nothing at all. When the bad weather came, and
it came at times, before it had even arrived the man would already be homeless. And in that squeezing of the house between
the waves and the trees, he never managed to learn what it was
that first pulled the house down, whether the dashing of the
waters or the beating of branches that covered the house as the
wind shook them. Luckily for him, the house would fall apart as
soon as the storm began to be felt, for otherwise, stuck between
the waves and the tree trunks on that tiny narrow strip, he
would be carried off by the highest waves that would come later,
or the tree trunks, beating against one another, would smash his
head. So it was that as soon as the cabin—a weak construction of
sticks and some leaves and algae—looked as though it were

going to fall, the man left it, walked along the small strip of
sand and sat down further away, on a great cape that entered into
the sea. There he waited patiently while the storm increased,
pretended that it would end the world, and then subsided completely. The cape was very large and entered far into the sea, yet
the sea could not even reach its peak, for it was very high; and
since, furthermore, it was of stone, a very hard stone, no trees or
grass took root there. It might seem as though, since the cape
was like that, it was a fitting place for the man to put up his
house, and not in that narrow little spot between the forest and
the sea. But the man didn't like the cape; he thought it hard, too
high, inaccessible to the waters and impenetrable to the roots.
Or perhaps he didn't even think of this—what is certain is that
he liked the other spot, and there, after patiently waiting on the
cape for the storm to end, he would return to construct his tiny
cabin. And, because he liked the spot, it was there that he
wished to be always. It couldn't be said that no one knew why he
lived alone on that spot, for no one knew that he did live there.
And how had he come there? By ship? Through the forest? Had
he been shipwrecked? Had he fallen from the sky, from a plane
that had passed overhead? Not even he himself knew, and if he
had known it once, he had meanwhile forgotten. And what did
he live on? Sometimes, on a fish that he fished or caught unexpectedly on the sandfloor, in the limpid transparency of the
waters that looked like blue glass. Other times, on a bird or a
monkey that got lost and came out of the forest and, finding
itself free before the sea, could not locate a passageway among
the palms, the branches, the vines, and the big and small leaves
that were like a green wall facing the blue of the water. He
scaled them, or plucked them or skinned them, and afterwards
roasted them on an iron spike that he had and that was the only
furnishing of his house and the only thing he took with him
when he went up to the cape to wait patiently for the storm
to pass.

The man was not old. Tall and vigorous, much burned by the sun and hardened by the rains and the sea wind, he amused himself by climbing the trees or swimming in the sea, or he would remain seated on the sand, at the cabin's door, with his feet almost in the foam that reached him, looking at how the sky changed color and, with the color of the sky, the sea changed its blue. Or he would look at the waves shining in the distance, spreading out on the sand or beating against the cape, and listen to the sounds that came from the forest, the yelps of monkeys and singing of birds, or the mere murmurings of the leaves on the trees in which the breeze got entangled. He was not often happy, even though at times he would sing. Neither was he sad. Yet at night, when there was no moon silvering the sea and the cape and the outlines of the trees in the forest, because it was a new moon, or because heavy clouds, thick and dark, covered a full or waxing or waning moon, if he lingered a while longer at the cabin door he felt a kind of delicate sadness and his eyes overflowed with a few tears. But he was not sad, no. Nor did he even talk to himself. When he would talk, speech for him was generally a kind of forceful addition to the work of his hands, or an imaginary conversation with the animals he caught in order to eat, while he tried to catch them or, after having caught them, while he scaled, plucked, or skinned them. But he did almost no work at all, and one animal lasted him for more than a day. So he did not have occasion to talk much, and otherwise he almost never remembered speech. It so happened that, though they were rare, seabirds would sometimes appear fluttering by and would settle on the high cape where they could croak, caw, chirp with one another, or remain there, immobile and silent— black, beaked, and white-breasted. With those that came from he knew not where, and that left as they had come, not even making a nest in the hard rock of the cape, a smooth and harsh rock, angular but without any hidden hollows where one of the birds could lay an egg; with these, yes, he somtimes wanted to

talk. Especially when, immobile and silent, or pecking at the
feathers beneath their wings, they looked at him sideways,
barely making him out at the cabin door, close to the sea, in the
narrow fringe of sand that ended at the cape, and then his voice
would rise to his mouth to question, to speak. But they were
seabirds, with guttural, raucous, jolting voices, and they did
not speak, nor did he have occasion to eat them, ever since the
time a gull or albatross or sea raven, its wings broken, had fallen
in the sea almost at his feet and he had plucked it and roasted it
on the spike. The hard and brackish flesh, very dark and sinewy,
had not agreed with him. When there were storms and he went
up the cape, the birds were there with him, huddled against the
stone, patiently waiting for the storm to subside. In the light of
fireflies he saw them; but, since at that point he and the birds
were concerned only with waiting, with resisting the wind and
the rain, no camaraderie had been established between them.
Coming from he knew not where and disappearing above the
waters just as they had come, they were in fact the only living
beings to whose presence he had grown accustomed, and they
appeared to him to be ever the same ones. Surely they were not.
Some would never return again, once they had left; others who
came, had perhaps never before been there—which was all the
more likely as, in that hard and angular rock with no hollows,
none had made a nest. Nor, for that matter, were they many at
the same time; and surely they stopped there by chance, en route
to other capes or merely to rest from the endless chase that,
suspended over the sea with sharp eyes, in rapid dives they gave
to the fish they sighted. From them the man had learned something: that way of hovering attentively, of diving suddenly, of
catching a fish with his hands or on the point of his spike, just as
they did in their long and sharpened beaks with curved tips.
Not that he hovered in the air and let himself fall, obviously;
but he would float and then dive, or, standing in the quiet

water, would spot fish that trusted enough in his immobility to swim near him.

Precisely on a day when he was floating with his spike in his fist, he saw pass by, a bit slowly, lurching between two waves, a form that, looking again, he saw was a fish. A large and strange fish, which seemed to have paws instead of fins, or a pair of paw-like fins, with a shiny and whitened, very round body that looked covered with feathers. It was a fish he had never seen, not in all those years he had lived there on that small narrow strip between the sea and the forest. The fish went this way and that, rose, descended, went a bit further that way, stopped and, with its head to one side, kept on looking at him. They stayed thus for some time, he surprised at the fish's watching him and without it occurring to him to dive and throw his spike, and the fish very calmly looking at him with its round and bluish eye edged in red. The man, then, slowly dove. The fish did not move. The man came to the surface to breathe, still slowly, without any splashing. And then he again put his head in the water and looked. The fish had not moved, as far as he could tell, and continued to look at him with the same wide-open eye. The man gently swam a few lengths and looked again. The fish had accompanied him, had even surfaced a little, and had stopped to look at him fixedly. The man was intrigued, not certain of what to do and no longer even thinking of catching the fish, which seemed not to know that there ever had been someone who had once considered catching it. The man was not far from the land, the waves were calm and broad. He swam slowly toward the beach and once in a while immersed his eyes to see the fish that, without a doubt, a little further down, between two waves and off to one side, was accompanying him, always staring at him with its round blue eye edged in red. It even made one or another awkward turn with some sudden movements of its paw-fins, and then calmly resumed its way, which was the same as the man's in the direction of the beach. Close to the beach, when he was already able to stand, the man felt a sudden pain in his side and sat on the ground, in that swaying and floating manner of a dreamer walking in water. And he was about to continue walking along with the small intermittent waves, when he felt something smooth and soft rub against his legs, almost making him fall. He stopped, and he saw that the fish, in successive turns and counterturns haltingly made by motions of its paw-fin, was rubbing against his legs in a friendly way, so content that it did not even raise toward him its wide-open blue eye, of a blue paler than the sea on a clear day. The man, in a surprise that was astonishment and almost worry, hurried somewhat, and even splashed the waters that were barely breaking on the small strip of narrow sand on which his house stood. He lost sight of the fish among the light foam and the rising sand, and only when he stood on the beach did his eyes search for it. He did not see it and, alongside but out of the water, he could not see it because the waters spread out, shining thickly, and nothing that was in them could be discerned from there. Thus he stood for some time, thinking of the fish, and then, no longer thinking of the fish, he let himself remain there forgetfully, looking at the edge of the water where he had stood when the fish had offered him its caresses. Night fell. What fish could that be? Indeed, only because it swam beneath the water did it seem like a fish. If it moved above the water, on its surface, judging by the kind of feathers (they were feathers without a doubt) that covered it, by the fins that looked like feet, by the hints of fin that seemed to be wings, by its lurching and vacillating way of moving, it would be a duck. It was therefore a duck-fish. A duck-fish, half fish and half duck, but in the end more duck than fish; it was an animal that he had never seen, that he did not know, nor did he know that he had ever heard of such a thing. But that there existed at least one, that this one had appeared to him and had even liked him, of this there could be no doubt. Or could it be a dangerous animal, which approached its victims that way? What possible reason could the duck-fish have for liking him, when he, with his spike in hand, could go catch it like any other fish?

On the following days, since no monkey or bird came out of the forest, he returned to the sea, caught some fish, but, though he always stayed quietly floating and scanning the transparent interior of the clear water with his eyes, the duck-fish did not appear. Then, because birds came from the forest, and once a monkey, for several days he did not return to the water. One day he went back to what he called fishing. He caught several fish and waited for the duck-fish, but it did not appear. Days passed then on which, walking into the water, he found not even one fish, days on which neither birds from the forest nor monkeys, nothing, fell into his hands. He did not go hungry, for in the compact vegetation that created a green wall at the seashore there were always fruits that he could eat. But he wanted a fish, especially a certain one, neither big nor small, with golden scales, a flattened and curved body, that he liked very much and that was, moreover, the kind he most often found. A kind of catch that was prettier than the others and flatter than they. But it seemed as though all the fish had given out, even the duck-fish. There were many such days. Until one day he was floating over the water with his eyes looking into it, having even forgotten about the duck-fish, when he felt something fluffy and soft rub against his belly. He bent suddenly, ceasing to float, and excitedly dove in. As soon as he returned to the surface and floated again, he looked and saw the duck-fish, a little below and to one side of him, very quietly staring at him with its wide-open blue eye, and in its mouth that seemed like a bill it held one of those fish that he most liked. The duck-fish then came close to his hands and face, let go the other fish that was half dead, and moved away in that lurching and shaky swim that was its own; but it stopped further on, turned toward him, and looked at him with its wide-open eye edged in red. The man reached out his hand and grabbed the fish that the duck-fish had visibly offered him. And then the duck-fish came and gently rubbed itself, fluffy and soft, against his belly and his legs that were hanging a bit in the water. When it passed close to his hand that held not the fish but the spike, with the back of his hand and his arm the man caressed the duck-fish which immediately made an awkward half turn and itself came to rub up against his arm. So they stayed for a long time, the man amused with giving caresses, and the duck-fish content to receive them and not even raising its rounded and blue gaze to him. Then the man moved in the direction of the beach and, when he was close enough, stood up in the water and waited. He soon felt the duck-fish, soft and fluffy, beginning to rub against his legs, making slow and awkward turns, passing between his legs, circling now one leg, now the other. The man let himself be and every so often immersed his head to observe the fish turning. He then lifted one leg, and he expected that, while he was walking toward the land, the fish would go on wanting to caress him, as it had done when he had nearly been startled. He took a step, and then another, and still another. But he did not feel the fish rubbing against him. He tried to see it, and made out that the fish was moving along at his side, at a distance that did not inhibit his steps. The man was already so close to his house that, with a brusque gesture, he threw toward it the fish he was carrying and the spike that was his only possession. And then, lowering himself and placing his hands in the water, he made a motion as if to take hold of the duck-fish, which, though without hurrying, moved away a little. The man advanced toward it and again extended his hands. This time the duck-fish came and let itself be caught. It was very heavy, much heavier than the man expected, and, though he was very strong, only with great effort did he manage to lift it into his arms, like someone setting a child in his lap. So the fish remained, outside the water and in his arms, but it did not struggle; rather, it purred, throbbed slightly, and with eyes closed rested its head on his arm, perfectly tranquil and satisfied. All at once, however, it began to arch and, as if against its will, to thrash about. The man understood that although it wished to, it could not remain so long out of the water, and he sat down on the sand, in the water, swept by the foam of the small waves that came up the beach, but with his arms immersed so that the duck-fish could stay within the element in which it could breathe. And with one of his hands, while the other arm cradled the fish, he rubbed it slowly, carefully, tenderly. He did not know how long they both stayed that way, but finally the fish, awkwardly, indicated that it wanted to free itself. The man released it in the water and the fish, after making a few circles near his torso, rubbing fluffily and softly, went away.

From then on rarely did a day pass that he did not go fishing and that the duck-fish did not appear to him carrying in its bill one of the fish that he most liked, offering it to him, and afterwards letting itself be caught so that, as the man sat at the water's edge, it would stay in his arms taking in the caresses that made it vibrate lightly and purr in satisfaction. If some time, for days on end, the fish did not appear, the man felt troubled and pained, dove in search of it, or remained pensive and watchful at the water's edge, his eyes fixed on the sea, awaiting a sign which the duck-fish, however, never gave, for it only appeared when he, floating in anticipation, lay suspended on the surface of the water above the blue transparency. And, when the duck-fish returned, bringing him in its bill his favorite fish, it was a joy for them both: they swam side by side, rubbing against one another, surfacing and diving, and it would invariably end with the man sitting on the sand, the duck-fish in his arms, caressing it, and the duck-fish purring, vibrating lightly, or very quiet in the water beside him, looking at him with its bluish eye, very rounded and edged in red.

One night, or rather one nightfall, when the man was about to go to sleep in his cabin—and never again, ever since the duck-fish appeared, had he felt on moonless nights a sadness come out of the shadows and fill him—he sensed that the cabin was collapsing on top of him. Immediately he got up and walked along the narrow little strip, between the sea and the forest, toward the cape. And he sat, almost lying down, making himself as comfortable as possible in the varied concavities of the rock, patiently to await the end of the storm. It, however, delayed its arrival, with numerous and diverse forewarnings such as strong gusts of wind, now from one direction, now from another, and violent downpours splashing about, and sudden stillnesses in the air during which the waves themselves seemed to hesitate in the silence and then merely rumble dully on. Along the cape, at a fair distance from the man, very few seabirds had taken shelter and they clung to the rock in small groups, cawing or croaking or chirping, but as if in fear, almost in a trill that softened their shaking, raucous and guttural voices. From time to time, above all at those moments when the air hung suspended, a shiver ran through the groups, very lightly, and only one or another of the birds, in the anxious immobility in which they stood, made a frustrated gesture of raising a wing and pecking beneath it. When the gusts of wind returned, a crackling thundered in the air, immediately followed by an immense echo that was a humming, rumbling, howling tremor of everything including the cape itself. The birds were quiet, and once when a bolt of lightning swept the sky and the sea, not followed by any thunder, the man, seeing the birds lower their heads silently, like someone waiting for a blow from which he cannot flee, remembered the many times he had wanted to converse with them and how, ever since the duck-fish had appeared to him, he had never again had such a thought, though he did not talk to the duck-fish. It was then that flashes of lightning covered the sky, crisscrossing in all directions, and a sudden blackness filled the air, the forest, the sea, and the cape, and in the thunder that rolled again and again could be heard a hissing that intensified, changed into a rumble, a crackling, a beating intermittently repeated above one continuous sound, and the gale and the rain fell vertically. The man felt a shapeless weight crush and whip him; it seemed to dismember, disembowel, dissolve him, and he felt, more than saw, immense sheets of water that were broken waves rise repeatedly against the cape and then plunge downward in the wind and the crashing rain. How long was he like that? Clinging how? He could not say, nor could he have ever imagined, for at times the wind seemed to come, in a wave of rain, from the very mass of the cape, raising the entire cape and he with it, or lifting him from the stone to which he clung. Days? Hours? Only instants? He hardly noticed when the storm ended. Upon opening his eyes, or even before opening them, he stirred, in a vague early morning warmth that penetrated his bones, and his whole body noticed the change that had occured.

He got to his feet. From the cape to the horizon, as far as the eye could see, an immense stretch of sand yellowed the serene and blue edge of a still dark sea, and the forest was a green wall far away, far from the cape and the sea, but a wall that, observed more carefully across the distance, at last grew in height, with enormous openings through which sand could still be seen. The man stood there watching: now the cape where not even one bird remained, now the sea over which coarse foam came and went, breaking with a screech of successive waves scattering on the beach, now he again watched the immense smooth stretch of sand, yellowed as far as he could see. Slowly he went down from the cape which was now very low on the side of the beach, and he walked on the sand, a fine, moist, swept sand, at the foot of which a kind of breeze was shifting sand that was finer still and dry and here and there whitened the yellow sameness of the immense beach. The sun, in a cloudless blue sky made rosy by the dawn, traced at his feet a slender shadow whose contours fluttered in the groping breeze. And the man, having taken a few hesitant and absorbed steps, stopped, aware that in the midst of such a change he did not even know the location of the cabin he had lived in for so long and which he had easily reconstructed so many times. He then walked obliquely to the edge of the water that, as limpid foam in which only fine sand was suspended, came coldly to lick at his ankles. And looking at the sea, which seemed to him the same and yet other, he remembered the duck-fish. Actually, he had always remembered it, throughout the storm; and after, when he still lay on the rock with eyes closed; and while he had looked at all the changes; until this moment in which, at the water's edge, it was precisely the duck-fish that he recalled in a deep sadness, as deep as all that had changed. Despite the cold that he began to feel, more from the immense desolation of the beach than from the luminous sun of the calm dawn little by little becoming morning, he proceeded into the sea and swam slowly, diving attentively, and following the stiff dark waters in one direction and the other, now floating, now swimming, in search of his fish. Thus he stayed until the sun had passed its zenith, but the duck-fish did not appear. He returned to the beach, walked a few steps along it, and lay down on the sand to rest. He felt infinitely exhausted. Perhaps he even slept an agitated sleep, peopled by wide-open eyes that passionately stared at him, edged in red, and from which he awoke twisting on the sand, feeling on his belly, his hips and his legs the memory of a fluffy and soft grazing, and in his arms, against his heaving chest, a lightly vibrating purring. He got up, entered the water which had quieted now into an even deeper transparency that only some far-off foam disturbed, there where the winds came down upon the sea, and again he swam, swam, swam, and floated and dove, searching for the fish, waiting for it, in a restless, desperate yearning. At times he thought he saw the awkward white form emerge, other times he felt it rub against his legs and belly, soft and fluffy. He would dive then, eyes wide open, but he could not, could not see the fish.

Days and nights, nights and days, he lived like that, now exhausted on the sand, now lurching into the sea, now swimming and diving, now dragging himself up the beach, now letting himself fall so near the tide that the foam wrapped him gently in his sleep and, like a balm that he accepted without care or anguish, seemed to him to be the purring of the fish, and its soft and fluffy tenderness, against his belly, his hips, his back, his whole body. He would turn then with eyes closed and absorb, through his scorched, salty, and smooth skin, or through his nostrils along with the bitter smell of the fine and salted sand, veering his head slowly from side to side, he would absorb this presence the idea of which enveloped him but that no longer came to greet him. And it was at this time that he began to wander interminably along the beach, now and then entering the sea again and lingering, in a desperate and melancholy search. And he stayed away, day and night, from the cape that had been the border of his narrow strip of sand and that was now a vague grey form entering into the sea, at the end of an expanse of beach where the marks of his steps and of the places where he had fallen dreaming were slowly disappearing in the continual polishing that imperceptibly merged tide and wind in the same constant and continuous whisper.

One afternoon, when he was sitting on the sand and distractedly contemplating the sea, resting from that fatigue that overcame him after searching the waters and roaming along the vast beach, he saw, coming from the blue sky in which only fine white clouds formed a dispersed and vaporous dust, a black dot and another and another, and then more, so that when the last could hardly be made out, the first were already seabirds, fluttering in a circle above him, in the fixed silence of hovering wings marred only by one or another chirp, a cawing of a beak, an attentive and restful croaking. He let himself fall back in order to see better. They seemed to him bigger than those that used to come to the cape, there where he had lived in the cabin built on a narrow strip between the forest and the sea. How distant it all was! He saw their black claws retracted, settled against their white bellies, and their necks that suddenly curved when they hovered back and seemed to turn toward him, at the same time, their gaze and their half-open beaks. Then he noted that, strangely, it was not really toward him that they looked. In fact, the circles that they formed as they flew above him in levels were not centered on him. A jolt, a strange jolt rang through him and ended as a restlessness in his feet. A dizziness blackened the air before him. He rose suddenly, or it seemed to him sudden in the slowness of his extreme weakness. And he distinguished, at the edge of the spraying foam that was coming to rest up on the beach, and not very far from where he was, a rounded white form, like a drowned hen that the tide had left behind. He ran lurching toward it. A chorus of raucous caws, of sharp and husky chirps, burst into the air. But he barely heard them for he was already kneeling, trembling and smiling, with tears running down his face and a cold sweat leaving pearls on his forehead, and taking the duck-fish into his arms. With its little touches of fins that looked like languid wings, and its fins that looked like feet, hanging loosely, the half-opened bill, and the white feathers that seemed dingy and frizzy, the fish lay with eyes closed, making no motion, not purring, doing nothing. Almost with a leap the man threw himself into the water that splashed and whirled about them, and then emerged and sat down like the other times, caressing the fish as he held it beneath the water. He rocked it, he pressed it against his chest, he shook it with fury, he smoothed out its frizzy feathers, but the duck-fish remained languid, making no motion, not opening its eyes. The man, absorbed, grew agitated, at times raising his head to breathe when the scattered foam, amidst waves, lifted him up, and then sinking down again, skimming the sand without sitting on it. Thus they remained for a long time, and the man did not hear the cawing that in wide turns continued above his head, nor did he see that the circles were ever lower, slanting downward across the beach. Then a tremor ran through the duck-fish. And another, slower tremor, like a being that with immense effort ascends from its anchor in frightful and abysmal depths. And slowly, like someone raising a craggy and hard cliff, similar to the cape that in the distance could no longer even be made out, the fish opened its eyes, or rather the eye closest to the man, and stared at him bluishly, wide-openly, redly-edged, in a tremendous tenderness, lengthy, concentrated, and grateful. The man let out a howl which was a raucous rasping and a grating of teeth. The fish shivered, went stiff, went soft, closed its eyes, and then its paws, wings, and bill turned rigid, and its feathers frizzy and dingy with no luster and no softness, but dark and cloudy in the arms of the man who now heard the gentle tide around him, the birds chirping, and even a murmur of sand moving along the beach. It lasted only an instant. His head fell against his chest, and a wave of foam lifted him, held him hesitant between retreating or advancing, and the hair at the side of his head rose and fell within the water. Then the man seemed to want to get up, attempted a kind of shifting of his body, and went drifting slowly along, somewhat strangely in opposition to what appeared to be the movements of the water. In his arms he still held the duck-fish, whose feathers now grew smooth as they calmly floated, regaining their sheen and even their softness. Little by little, however, the duck-fish disentangled itself and went drifting too, but on a different course. Against the ruby greenness of a pure sunset, the birds were black, silent, hovering parallel, very low, and some few came to rest on the beach, attentively following with a slight swaying of their necks that hesitant floating, adrift in the sea that was so transparent and blue that their shapes were tinged by iridescent streaks. The figures moved apart from one another, uncertain, and at times it seemed that the current was bearing them toward the deep, and then again that the wide waves of the calm tide would finally deposit them on the sand.

Thus night fell. As a vague gleam of light began to spread throughout the sky, giving the sea a greyish tone in which there was a menacing hint of a chill that was not even a breeze, a small bright mass, and another longer and darker one, appeared on the beach, at the edge of the water that, against the misty pallor of the sand, was an undulating blackness barely tinged with the whiteness that only from time to time skimmed by them. From the sea, or from further up on the beach, or even from the edge of the water, they could hardly be seen. But even so the birds that had emerged from the depths of the whitened horizon that turned yellow at the foot of the sea soon saw them, distant from one another. A black dot and another and another, and then more, and they were finally enormous and silent birds, the first fluttering in a circle while the last could hardly be made out, dot by dot, in the distance. A few settled on the sand and cawed softly, staring attentively at the two figures, with their heads at an angle. The others continued hovering silently, in circle upon circle, observing the man who, on his back, with his arms in a vague gesture of embrace and his legs spread apart, seemed to stare at them with his eyes wide open, and the duck-fish, further away, stretched out and gleaming. It was then that one of the birds fell like a stone and gouged out one of the man's eyes and rose again, and at once another fell, also like a stone, and gouged out his other eye and ascended. Two birds, among those resting on the sand, opened their wings, flapped them and took flight. One, which had skimmed away across the waters, turned directly back to the duck-fish and buried its beak in the base of its neck, while the other rose almost vertically and, descending suddenly in a spiral, with its beak open, in a single blow sheared the man's sex. As one group of birds would descend, crossing paths with the group that was rising, those that continued to hover in a circle chirped and dropped down too; but all of them, those that were rising and those that in two waves were dropping, in the end remained a hovering mass, a mass that cawed and collided with one another hanging in the air, very close to the man and the fish. Day was dawning, a red orb arose from the sea and soon spread across the line of the horizon on both sides. In a crackling of wings and cawing, the birds rose almost vertically and hovered, clustered in a very large circle. From the duck's neck, from the man's eye sockets and the coarse blackness where his sex had been rooted and his testicles still hung half sheared by the same blow, there trickled a thin liquid, vaguely bloodied, of which only a few diluted threads seemed to reach out toward the last of the foam approaching the bodies, and would linger in the foam as it receded. In successive spirals the birds swooped.

1959                              *Translated by Daphne Patai*

# Sea of Stones

For one can think that something
exists in such a way that it is not
possible to think it does not exist.
*Anselm of Canterbury,* Proslogion

*N*IGHT was falling. It had rained heavily. The road
between the high dripping hedges was a quagmire and in the
puddles a pallid sky reflected paler still. Gusts of wind moved
through the hedges shaking off drops of water and blew out
through the fields on a deserted plain, broken only now and
again by a dark, wind-tousled tree where limbs and branches
tenuously clutched a ragged, moving mist. The figure hurried
haltingly along his way, laboriously moving around puddles and
avoiding the mud. Leaning on a staff, his steps were uncertain,
faltering, as of one who in the growing darkness had trouble
seeing the ground; his staff groped on, managed by infirm fists.
No house was visible in the surroundings, no hovel, nothing.
Not even flocks. No horseman rode along. And the dark, rustic
night enveloped the figure who, at a certain point, stopped.

He did not raise his head to look around or search the
horizon. He would rest a bit, perhaps, sure of his way although
less so of the night that mingled with the solitude, fast becoming one. He seemed to listen.

Was it a sound he heard above the intermittent whistling
of the wind, above the rustling of the hedges?

His face, alert and concentrated, was that of an old man, wreathed in dishevelled white hair; his blinking eyes held a faraway gaze and a vague smile lined his lips, deepening creases and wrinkles in his dry, pink skin. He wore a long friar's habit that reached almost to the muddy sandals on his thin, bony feet. He seemed to be waiting.

But whom would he encounter out there? Bandits on the road? And could an old friar be afraid of them?

Grasping his staff, immobile, with his robe fluttering in the harsh wind, thus he stood for a long time as the night fell almost completely.

He listened and waited. It was not uncommon for voices to speak to him. Nor was it his habit to seek them out, his self disciplined in those uncertain matters. At times it happened that everything inside him stopped and his spirit hovered, like that of God moving upon the waters. Things did, in fact, happen that way, for in anticipation of such an immobilization of his inner self, there was no hint, no sign, no thought; only the slightest bit of reticent and fearful curiosity which, if he was writing, would grip him, pen raised above the parchment, or, if he was praying in his cell, would give him the sensation that his knees no longer rested on the *prie-dieu*. Once, in the monastery church, he was overcome with embarrassment when his old friend, Friar Athelstan, upon seeing that he did not rise to hear the Gospel read, touched his habit and the habit crumbled to the floor with no one inside. The memories came back to him: he had been distracted only momentarily, absorbed in the con-templation of the copies of historical documents that he had received the previous day. Yet he had been perfectly able to feel the touch on his sleeve and was unaware that he was not there. The episode soon became famous and only the abbot's esteem for his scholarly disposition and incessant labors had spared him the scandalous notoriety that would have brought pilgrims and devotees to disturb the peace of mind of a soul who always wrote, always read, debated always, inquired always.

When everything stopped within, it was as if he heard a celestial music—with neither instrument nor choir, but music. And the voices that he would then hear were not really voices. They had nothing in common with the mental reading, etched methodically into the memory, which became his thought as he wrote his treatises, his *Ecclesiastical History;* nor with the sudden, inarticulate flashes that became words in his mouth at times when he was discussing points of doctrine with his students. But without a doubt he did hear voices. Only words seemed such paltry things, as did even the music of intuitive alliterations, for expressing the fullness that overtook him.

Of late, he had concluded his life's great work, and God had granted him sight almost to its conclusion. He had worn out his eyes in many years of study, but he had erected a monument to Britannic Christianity, exhausting his materials completely so that up to the present there was no martyrdom, synod, pilgrimage, founding of a convent, war or invasion that was not carefully registered. He had read thousands of documents, had interviewed hundreds of persons, had recorded minutely an era, rebellious, tumultuous, overflowing with piety and paganism which, like the waves of the sea, had beaten upon the portals of his Jarrow monastery, which he had entered as a young lad when the walls of the buildings were still being raised. Like the walls and with them he had grown in the order of Saint Benedict. But Adamnan of Iona, Aldhelm of Malmesbury, the Archbishop Theodore of Tarsus, his teacher Benedict Biscop, those who had encouraged the writing of so great a work—all were dead now. And Wynfrith was in Germany, occupied with converting the people and rebuilding the empire of the Romans.

The work done, he commended himself to God. But, in

the meantime, when he realized that he had concluded his *History* at the moment when the Arabs, invading Africa, which had been Augustine's, and Osorio's and Isidore's Spain, had been decisively stopped in Poitiers by the son of Herestal, he had seen therein, for the first time in his life of sixty serene years, a sign of the will of God, a kind of sanction, an epilogue, which, of course, did not prevent him from continuing to await with the greatest impatience a summary of the *Book of Amulets* by Prince Khalid of Damascus, an Arab, the disciple of that Marianus of Alexandria whom Adamnan had met in his travels to the Holy Land.

He had never been very far from Jarrow. Everyone else travelled so much! There were Scots everywhere, there were Greeks in London attracted by the Archbishop Theodore. But his Holy Land was the Jarrow cloister, the broad pavement under which so few friars slept the eternal sleep (Friar Athelstan already lay sleeping there, forever relieved of the palsy that afflicted his hand, which would rise in the air, as if to touch his habit, when he chanced upon his friend), his cell with the little narrow window, the arches of the church firmly atop the thick columns among which he and the other boys used to hide from their teachers. He would leave only to preach in the nearby villages or for a journey to Canterbury (and rarely had he travelled there). He preached very badly, he knew. His own preoccupations would constantly meddle in his sermons, and sometimes he spoke of things that no one understood; other times, distressed with the process of evangelizing his audience (it was well known that at night the people worshipped stones, although by day they believed in all manner of miracles), he resorted to simple stories from among the very many he knew concerning Anglo-Scottish saints or the martyrs from the persecutions.

But the persecutions were not his forte, and he grew dissatisfied with himself when he spent too much time on them.

Those horrors, that mutual ignorance, that veritable aversion to the beauties of science, to the delights of the Bible that Celsus had mocked, or those of Lucretius and Virgil whom the great Pope Gregory had despised—these did not blend with his dream of a virtuous, intelligent, educated Christianity, capable of appreciating, as did he, the poems of Caedmon, the riddles of Aldhelm, or even Lucretius, whom Biscop had warned him against reading, so atheistic, so materialistic! But had anyone ever described better than that pagan the dignity of a wise man or the flippant egoism of a man who, safe on the shore, feels happy not to be the one, far out to sea, attempting to defend a precarious life against the waves?

Now he could no longer read, he could no longer write. And his favorite secretary, Egbert, whose voice in Latin was like crystal and whose hand never erred, had been sent to York, and it was almost certain that he would replace the archbishop. But a great school was being organized in York, plans were well along, the seeds he had sown would not be in vain.

Would the peace the country now enjoyed be long lived? Who could foresee? Could history foresee the purposes of God? That problem troubled him always. He had already dreamed once of the sacking and destruction of Jarrow after his death. In the dream, he arose from the grave and harangued the invaders who, to judge by their horned helmets, were pirates from the North. And the invaders, whose loud laughter had awakened him in a cold sweat, threatened to bury him alive since, like Lazarus, he was then alive again.

He would not reach the village by day. The wind was rising. A fine rain began that made him quicken his pace in the trek which he had absently resumed, thinking of the travels of Adamnan. How he had delayed his departure! He almost never preached in the village without becoming lost in thought on the return trip. Rain or shine, winter or summer, he would always find himself out in the country—neither village nor convent in sight—and with no idea where he was. But there was no way he could arrive by daylight. Never had he left so late. He should not have come alone, nor should he have insisted that he had no need of the company of a novice to give him an arm and compensate for the defects of his eyes and his uncertain hands. He was stubborn, very stubborn, he ought to pray to God to forgive his stubbornness. All this was old age, of course; the delusion that one is as strong as ever. And he had never been strong. Hadn't he? What ailments had he suffered? None! And in his youth, Benedict Biscop—God rest his soul—had punished him many times for his absorption in games and contests, and the truth is that he had been the champion foot racer for two years.

He tripped and fell. The path was a swamp in which he sat mired. Groping, he searched for his staff. And could not find it. The cold, the water, the darkness, penetrated him. Before succumbing to his own concern and worry over the worry that his absence would cause in the monastery, he knelt in the water and prayed. On such occasions he always said a prayer that he had composed in Latin verse, meticulously styled, inspired by Boethius whose *Consolation* was his favorite book. But, in spite of it all, he could not resist smiling, inwardly, at the disproportion between his situation and that of the minister of Theodoric. Who could cut his head off?

And at that very instant, a blade glistened above him.

"Wait!" said a voice.

"Why?" asked another.

The friar arose. "My sons, which of you will find my staff?"

"It is our father," said the first voice. And the second laughed.

"Father," said the second voice, "give us the thirty pence you got for the ox you sold in the village."

"My ox is that of the Evangelist," said the friar, "and I have never sold it for the price of Judas."

"He is a friar from the convent," said the voice that had

called him "father" as a joke. "He is one of those to whom the King gives everything, leaving nothing for us."

The friar closed his eyes, said a *pater noster* and a Hail Mary for his soul, because it was true, the youth were abandoning the country for lack of employment. The King was giving everything to the religious houses, it was not worth being a loyal servant if one could not earn what a master must give as reward to those who seek to serve him.

"Are you off to other kingdoms, my sons?"

"We are," said the first voice, "for you eat up everything that is ours."

"No," the friar answered firmly, "neither I nor my monastery. But you will lose your soul over the anger that is in you."

"If we serve the King and he pays us poorly, and our souls are filled with anger, it is not our souls that will be lost but his, just as you were about to lose your head," answered the first voice.

"My sons," said the friar, "I am old and almost blind. Which of you will find my staff? And remember that to harm a man of the cloth would be your eternal perdition. For that reason alone I ask you: do not harm me. I pardon you and give you my blessing, for truly you are not guilty. They never spoke to you as sons, they never paid you as men, they never treated you like angels. And man, created in the image and semblance of God, is a son because he was born of the flesh, is a man because God gave him a soul, and is an angel when the Holy Spirit enlightens him."

"Father," said the first voice, "take your staff and we will travel with you. Here it is."

The friar began to walk in their midst, speaking continuously, unaware that he was speaking. And at one point, as he was stating that the Kingdom of God was not of this world but that men must live in the world, and that the friars were intermediaries between the Kingdom of God and that of the world, because they took on themselves the sins of the world yet were separated from it by their vows, the rain became so heavy that one of the youths said:

"We can't keep on like this. Let us seek some sheltered place to spend the night. I'm soaked to the bone, we can't see a thing, and we'll find no houses around here."

"Somewhere around here is that temple where the village women go lie upon a stone when they cannot conceive," said the one who saved the friar's neck from the other's sword.

"Those are terrible sins," said the friar, "things of the devil that should not be done. How can we take shelter there?"

"Excuse me," said the one with the sword, "but they do those things because they do not lie with me. Those that have slept with me have never come to sin on that stone!"

"But they sinned with you and you with them," said the friar. "Matrimony is a sacrament celebrated by the spouses and witnessed by the Church."

"Come now, Father, people do that sacrament alone, for these aren't things to be done in front of others, as animals do."

They had left the path and, speaking their blasphemous and immoral words, helped the friar accompany them through the sodden countryside where now, unlike when the friar had become distracted, stones were as numerous as their stumblings, if not more so. A mass of steep rocks loomed before them in the night, and it was the temple of which the young man had spoken. The friar knew the place; he had on various occasions inveighed against those acts that to him seemed monstrous. It had tall stones, in a circle, covered by one enormous stone. The wind pierced him, but, sitting off to one side, they were somewhat sheltered although shivering in their cold, wet clothing.

Then the friar spoke to them at length, minutely, of virtue, of chastity, of piety, of duty, which the lads acknowledged in sleepy or irritated apostrophes, confident that his poor eyesight and their situation would prevent him from recognizing them later. They no longer thought of killing him; nor did they even seem to remember that they had thought of doing so. At a pause in his placid exposition, the friar heard them snore. They had fallen asleep.

The friar began to think of how his life could have taken the direction of theirs, and how he had barely escaped losing the one he had, precisely at the moment in which he had thought of Boethius's beheading. What if he had not been taken as a child to the monastery; what if he had not been a handsome or docile child, as they said; what if he had encountered not good teachers but others who rejected him; what if . . .

He opened his eyes and it was day, a luminous day that struggled through the compact veil of a low fog. More than that he could not see when he moved to the entrance. He turned, and the two lads, both so young, were sleeping outstretched, with mouths half open, their faces serene and distant. He crouched to see them better, first next to one, then the other. One of them, who had the sword at his belt, was lying on the stone that the women would lie upon. The friar blessed them, and suddenly his hand traced the sign of the cross over each of them.

It was as if the sign had awakened them. They both yawned and, in the distraction that is the awakening of youth which seems always to be returning from far away, they sat up and looked around until, seeing the friar, they lowered their eyes, contrite and ashamed.

"My sons," said the friar, "it is daylight. Let us continue on our way."

And, taking up his staff, he started off.

"Father," said the one with the sword, "we did not come this way. The road is over there," and he pointed.

"All roads lead to Jarrow," said the friar, smiling, but he turned around and followed them, supported by his staff.

When they arrived at the roadway, all three stopped. The two lads, embarrassed, did not know what to say. The friar, with good words, bade them farewell and stood in the road watching them leave, in a hurried and yet uncertain manner, in the direction from which he had come. Suddenly, he called to them. They turned, suspended. The friar kept calling them until they came back to where he stood. Then the friar said to them: "My sons, I gave you only good words and now you will go out into the world. This cannot be. I am too old to go with you. You come with me."

The two looked at each other. And the one with the sword, because of what had transpired, said with a scornful smile, "Go with you where, Father? To the monastery? Only if the stones speak. Father, you do not know what life is. Only if the stones speak, like people, since people, Father, are like stones."

"They will speak," said the friar, and his eyes fled into the distance.

"Oh, will they? Then come here," shouted the youth. And, almost dragging the friar after him, he took him back to the old pagan temple.

On the gentle hill that sloped down to the other side, there was, extended almost out of sight, a sea of stones. Large ones, small ones, sharp ones, round ones, washed by the rain and the wind, with sparse vegetation growing between them, there were in fact a multitude of stones.

"Speak to them. They don't even know who you are."

And the friar spoke. He told of the creation of the world, of the tablets of the Law, of the prophet's tears, of the passion of Christ, of how He descended into limbo and resurrected from the dead, of how Peter had denied Him and had been the first Pope; he spun out the lives of saints, he discussed the *Etymologies* of Isidore and the *Confessions* of St. Augustine; he quoted Lucretius and Virgil and compared them with the *Song of Songs,* and then the *Aeneid* with the *Book of Job.* He described his childhood and his youth, expounded his philosophy of history, recalled friends, their works, the conversations he had had with them. And he ended by reciting his special prayer.

Seated at his feet, the two young men smiled perplexed, skeptical, annoyed smiles, irritated by so many ideas, so many thoughts, so much information, so many things that meant nothing to them. The old man's voice was not pleasant and his manner of speaking was dry and without grace.

Then the other pulled at the tip of his muddy and moist habit and said quietly, "Father, ask them if they understood you and if they liked your words."

The priest lowered his eyes to him and remembered how many times he had sought relief from the weight of his heart and the weight which in his heart made him know that his heart itself was insatiable.

"My children, my children! Have you understood me and have you liked what you heard?"

A crackle, a groan, a rumble sounded on the slope.

"Yes, Venerable Bede!" answered the stones in chorus.

Tears ran down the old man's cheeks and he felt his hands wet with tears and with kisses.

He lowered his eyes toward the two young heads, shaggy and unkempt.

"Let us go, my sons."

The three arrived at the roadway. There the friar raised his hand to bless them.

"A promise is a promise, Father. We will go with you," said the one with the sword at his waist.

"No, my sons. Go into the world with my blessing. I release you from your promise. What the stones understood, you will understand."

And, supporting himself on his staff, he began his journey back to the monastery.

The monks were astir with commotion. Everyone ran to meet him. Thieves? Brigands? Had he stayed in the village? Where had he been?

Bede smiled with a vague look in his eyes and said nothing. Then the abbot himself touched his sleeve to rouse him. The habit crumbled to the floor before the eyes of the entire community. Where, at that moment, was Bede?

1960                              *Translated by Christopher C. Lund*

# The Corner Window

It is enough that it burns in so noble
a fire; it is enough that I have been
raised to the sky and delivered from
the ignoble number.
*Giordano Bruno,* The Heroic Frenzies

$D$ONA Felisberta Henriques's grandmother was named
Berta. She had died young, almost suddenly, leaving in the
family memory the image of a kind of a fragile veil which, until
torn by a gust too strong for such delicate fabric, had protected
from adverse winds the sons and husband capable only of rous-
ing those winds, never of calming them. In Dona Felisberta's
perpetually darkened sitting room, duplicated in the gilt-
framed mirror whose steel was obscurely flaking in the dimness,
hangs the portrait of "unhappy Berta," in the sarcastic expression of the deceased Henriques who, while mistreating in his
turn his own wife, never forgot to compare grandmother and
granddaughter, based on the horoscopic games of his father-in-
law, the youngest son of the aforementioned lady whom he knew
only by means of that portrait, so odious in its useless immensity and so vulnerable to comparisons devoid of all imagination.
And in very little were they, grandmother and granddaughter,
comparable. Physically, Dona Felisberta even when young had
lacked that vague and melancholy charm of Berta absorbed in
the last poem in the album (in its leather cover with painted

flowers, that album lay in one of the dressing-table drawers, among the empty perfume and medicine bottles, dirty handkerchiefs, scattered letters, hairpins, old pictures from her girlhood, which provided the contents—carefully piled up in disarray—of all Dona Felisberta's drawers), that oblong face, with large eyes and a mouth that seemed about to open, those black and lustrous tresses parted in the middle and covering each ear, that calm bosom so vehemently rosied by the artist, or those arms, thin as in reality and yet rounded by the brush, which emerged from the richly green and puffed half-sleeves. And whether or not there was any resemblance—perhaps a timid and withdrawn reflection, altered by decades of other habits and harder lives—it would be unjust to bring the devouring and pallid flame, a bit mysterious and legendary, that had crushed the grandmother, near to the coals of the bourgeois brazier over which, to closed doors, the tenderness of the young Felisberta had slowly shriveled up, with no experience beyond her own painful discoveries and no children. She had loved badly, but faithfully and purely, the ardent speech and ample moustache of an Henriques whose sudden gestures and constraints would have shown her, had she then known how to see, the sum of coarseness and socks to be darned that they concealed.

One after another, in due or undue time, death had taken Dona Felisberta's uncles, aunts, and parents. With the habit of timidity and the pain of her wounded self-respect, she had cut or allowed to be cut ties of friendship with girls of her breeding, hoping to reduce to a minimum the number of witnesses to her domestic disappointment. Henriques, whether in the cruel quarrels with which he had worn out his wife or in the lusty peaces with which he would seal one more triumph of his liberty, had always lulled that thing resembling character which had slowly taken shape in Dona Felisberta, caused at the beginning by a timid withdrawal from an astonished ingenuousness set adrift in their married life, and later by the ever more vague ebb and flow of a scarred refusal to understand life. This character had been a latent possibility in an only daughter spoiled to distraction and without extensive company, or else an acquired taste in gentle revolt at a solitude with neither lucidity nor dignity which, moreover, Henriques, though he cultivated it, took pleasure in carelessly disturbing. So that, when death reappeared for a final stab at Dona Felisberta's dulled sentiments, and settled into their cursed marriage bed, her solitude grew complete as, once the unacknowledged feeling of relief had passed, it ever more densely circled and permeated an aging that had begun long ago, adding to distracted musings aloud and consolingly imaginative sham longings a certain sad curiosity about the doings of other people, in the street and among the neighbors, whom she contemplated through defects in the windowpanes on which hung curtains scorched by the sun in folds that had never been shifted but that now satisfied the curiosity, devoid of malice, with which Dona Felisberta liked to see without being seen.

Ever since a day when she had learned from the maid (at that time she had a maid) that her husband had become the lover of a neighbor in one of the buildings opposite her, whom he had set up on the very same block, Dona Felisberta had let the bolts rust on the windows of the utterly useless sitting room and confined herself, at that time fleetingly, to those facing the other street. The building was on the corner, with no right or left, having downstairs neighbors only, for the people upstairs had closed up their house and almost always stayed in the provinces. And even today, although they had been her contemporaries since time immemorial, Dona Felisberta treated these downstairs neighbors formally, waiting for them to go out or come in whenever she—and this only rarely—would meet them on her way in or out.

As time passed, Dona Felisberta had grown immobile at the corner window, by which she would sit in a low chair whose cane seat had aged along with her, had been polished by her, and from her alone took on the slightly sharp hollow of bony buttocks. There she remained not merely for hours, of which there were none in her solitary life, but for the revolving of the sun and the changing of the shadows, for the passage of creatures she never even got to know or await, for the rain that ran toward the gutters, bearing papers and debris, for the windows that opened, for others that closed, for the lighting of the lamps on the opposite corner, and, to the right of her horizon, the bit of the cul-de-sac which ended in that sudden yellow barricade, where some rare tufts of green submissively sprouted, holding back old newspapers that blew in the wind, when there was wind, but that Dona Felisberta had long watched in that unstable, fluttering position.

Seated in the small chair, Dona Felisberta was perfecting a lack of attention to the panorama that excited her curiosity, absorbed in some vague, interminable mending of old clothes fished out of her dresser and which had once been chemises, petticoats, bodices, bloomers, from an archaic and intimate wardrobe through which she had expressed her disillusionment with a sensuality that her husband imagined, in other women, adorned in fine, lacey, transparent weaves. Raising her eyes, awakened by some unusual movement or dark form, and shifting now one side, now the other, of the curtain, she commanded a vast and varied spectacle, if one could call vast that narrow crossroad in a far-off suburb, and if one could call varied the limited movement of those elusive streets whose very inhabitants—few simple folk and mostly comfortable burghers— ignored the street that was abandoned, in the still of night, to cats that calmly lived in the airshafts of the buildings and went out through openings near the floor to lick themselves at the edge of the sidewalk (Dona Felisberta paid them no attention, for she did not like cats), or to wandering young couples, looking for the alley with no way out where only one lamp, stupidly planted near the end, at night shone simply on the yellow barricade and cast lengthy shadows on the stones of the sidewalk and the walls of the nearby buildings.

The windows that looked out onto the other street had been abandoned by Dona Felisberta. Not that she had closed these up, any more than she had ever again opened the others, but because, facing the buildings opposite, the life that she glimpsed in them was too close to her, too visible, too much the same people always, for her not to secretly sense—although they had nothing to fear from a disinterested observation such as hers—that this life, out of disdain for the solitary old woman whom no one remembered to spy on, offered a contrast to the silent and calm isolation in which her own life seeped out. The corner window was different. From behind the windowpanes, with her chair positioned for implicit concealment with its back slightly toward the bit of street below the windows that would open (the wooden shutters were always open, for Dona Felisberta never closed them), but, through some already forgotten aversion, not facing fully toward the other street onto which the door of the building and the condemned windows faced, Dona Felisberta could follow with her eyes whoever might come from her left and go across to the blind alley, or from the street by her door and disappear beneath the limits of her horizon (formed by the window's edge and the possibilities of discretely moving the curtain), or, emerging from these borders, would cross the street, disappearing at the corner like a picture that gradually strays from its frame. The building opposite the crossroad was set apart from the four corners by having a grocery store downstairs that was the vital center of the neighborhood, though in the same diffuse and vague rhythm of scant persons that characterized the neighborhood and its residents. The sliding of the corrugated doors at day's end, for which the grocery boy would hang onto an iron pole that hooked into them, was one of Dona Felisberta's favorite episodes, as were also (and this motivated

her indistinct murmurs) the signs with changing prices stuck
into the sacks of potatoes, beans, and rice, which the corrugated
doors would hide until the next day. An occasional variant in her
observation consisted of wondering, without forcing her sight
or her imagination, if the change in prices corresponded to a
change in quality or merely to the gradual and inexorable rise in
the cost of living.

For Dona Felisberta the cost of living presented no problem. She lived on nothing. And, once a month, absorbed in her
fearful cares not to cross paths with the neighbors, and in a
phantasmagoric dream of the vehicles and commotion in the
center of the city, she went on foot, crossing numerous streets
after infinite hesitations, to collect the wretched pension that
Henriques had left her, the result of his obligatory deductions as
a civil servant, augmented beyond the obligatory by a false
foresight displayed among his colleagues. It was a paltry sum
from which, on the way back, dizzy also from the crowding and
the waiting with her ticket in hand and from the anxiety that
she would not hear them call her number, Dona Felisberta set
aside her usual rent. This, on her way home, she would leave at
an office above a store on Madalena Street, in whose wide and
gloomy entryway there would always be some wooden crates
containing dusty bundles and, in the corners, reeking of urine
tempered by the large ever-open doors, crumpled papers and
straw swept off the worn-out tiles that shone in the middle of the
entryway where the brightness of the street met the light that
came from a wide-open latticed window high above a stone
staircase flanked by ceramic tiles. Dona Felisberta would climb
the stairs, already taking out the money that she would hand
over to a bald man, a dark cigarette at the corner of his lip, who
sat at a desk in a small room at the back of a corridor lined with
rotting planks that sagged to one side owing to the age of
the building. Once she reached her street, after having crept
through multitudes that she could only distinguish when trans-

formed into selected figures by the framing of her windowpanes, Dona Felisberta would silently enter the grocery store and buy supplies for the month. Some potatoes, a few beans, some rice, a dozen eggs, plus this and that in exceedingly small doses that brought to the lips of the grocer an oblique smile of a man resigned to the meanness of the neighborhood. All this the boy would deliver later, with Dona Felisberta awaiting him so that he would not ring the bell which had disturbed her since the days when, placed there at Henriques's orders, and with an irritating timbre (softened now by the dust and by the insects that made their nest in it), the aggressive buzz seemed the very person of her husband who always insisted on ringing it as he would put his key in the door. Except for those rare mistakes by unknown people whom Dona Felisberta would watch, out of pure formality, through the grille in the door, and whom she saw looking around in the uneasy awareness that this was not the place they were seeking, only two other times each month did the bell ring. Then it was the bill collectors for the electricity and the water, for an almost symbolic charge, since Dona Felisberta hardly used light, and used no water at all on cleaning herself or the house, as part of the tacit program of abandon and neglect that, even during her husband's lifetime, she had been honing. In fact, in Dona Felisberta's house dust covered everything, not in successive layers but in a permanent continuity, filtered down by her relative immobility and by her habit of never opening the windows. A hint of garbage, encrusted and indistinct, was part of all the objects, of the color of the walls and the fabrics, and it gave off a bitter, musty odor which Dona Felisberta would have noticed, had she not contributed to it herself as well, had they not been in the end inseparable, in her surroundings and in her, the smell that came from the forgotten and closed up house and that emitted by her old body which hardly sweated and had not undressed completely in years, unless it was distractedly for some change in clothing that, without any apparent motive, had suddenly entered her sewing plans at the window ledge.

The knowledge that Dona Felisberta was acquiring of those who lived in the neighborhood or who passed beneath her eyes, or even of people who had established the occasional custom of stopping in those parts, was an uncertain knowledge that she did not deepen, as uncertain and as impersonal as her knowledge of the nits that slept cocooned in her grayed and dirty hair, or of the lice that wandered in it and sometimes, like the bugs in the vast wooden bed with chiseled legs, caused her a slight itch that in a light gesture, complacent and complicitous, she would scratch with the tip of her fingernail, alongside which her other fingers were raised in that curved gesture of delicacy with which, as a girl, she had learned to take hold of a teacup. Dona Felisberta did not individualize anyone, did not interpret, in the street or in the windows, any movement, made no conjectures about the day-to-day life or the destiny of those she observed. The repetition of certain hours coinciding with certain movements ended by being associated with a particular figure, by being identified with a turning on or off of the lights. In her memory, without thinking but with a precision that the passing of the years had sharpened, persons, gestures, movements, moments of light, sounds, at times clear, of a silent street, were bound to awaken particular recollections. In the form of fragments of dialogues that she persistently vocalized with a tremor of her drawn-back lips, or of flowing scenes that seemed to flit by, as if between her and her sewing, these recollections ever more distinctly referred to her youth, a youth in which she had not been young, nor in which she had ever been aware of having been young, but which was a suppression of the years lived with Henriques, an ever more luminous though not lucid landscape of the happiness that only on the eve of her marriage, in the conventional eagerness for domestic activity, she had managed to desire. These memories did not correspond to anything very precise, very experienced, very much imagined. With time, the transformation had occurred, as some persistent inner stubbornness, innocent and calming, had dissolved the pains and humiliations of her years as a married woman, suffered above all when, through a few acquaintances or relatives, she found some term of comparison for her pains and for her bridal yearnings. This transformation had turned her recollections into consolations, and clothed them in a prestige that bore no sting, fitted merely for the modest preoccupations of her spirit.

Little by little, at a certain point in her life, when evening fell, when the sun fled after merely grazing the grocery store corner, Dona Felisberta, alerted by slow movements turning the corner, shifted the curtain aside a bit and remembered, or rather was on the point of remembering, those times, few indeed, when she had thought of going for a walk in the afternoon with a beau. But her only beau had been Henriques, and an opportune itch or a broken thread made her release the yellowed curtain on the dirty glass.

How many days this was repeated, Dona Felisberta had no idea, but the truth is that it was repeated and, as the summer progressed, she touched the curtain ever more fleetingly, now that the neighbors above the grocery store spent the afternoons and evenings as if in a wide-open house, so exposed were the verandas on which they wandered in their undergarments, dragging their feet and leaning against the furniture, similar, in fact, to that in Dona Felisberta's dining room, where she, preferring the kitchen, never ate.

One afternoon, however, after watching the grocery boy kicking vigorously as he hung onto the hook in an effort to unleash the corrugated door which would not descend, she, remotely amused, forgot the neighbors and drew back the scorched curtain more than usual. At that moment she *saw herself* hand in hand with a slender figure, turning the corner in the direction of the blind alley. It lasted only an instant. Soon

she returned to her habits, let go the curtain, an itch assaulted
her, but only troubled and trembling did she manage to put one
more stitch into the sewing resting on her lap. She did not think
again of that vision until the moment when, as she pulled over
her body the grimy sheet and the quilt of multicolored patches
with a very frayed red fringe, she felt a pang, a slight ache, and
once again saw herself hand in hand with the slender figure. In
the shadows of her room the vision lingered, with no connection
to the past, completely independent and autonomous, though it
was neither exterior nor interior, not discernible in color or
shape, not describable in words. Dona Felisberta pulled the
bedclothes further up, snuggled into a strange well-being, and
fell asleep.

The following day, at the same hour, Dona Felisberta was
seated in her spot, half forgetful of the perturbations she had
felt, when the same pang as on the preceding night drew to her
attention that she was watching a young couple who had
stopped a bit beyond the grocery corner. She raised her hand to
the curtain, and sat there looking, and none of her vague pretexts kept her from an improper lingering. He was tall and
slender, his hips and groin arched forward, his back curved,
with a way of talking to the girl as if he stood obliquely over her,
his elbows seemingly detached from his body in a somewhat
suspended tension as he buried his hands in the pockets of his
trousers which, like his darker coat, were grey. He wore no tie,
and one of the edges of his shirt collar lay loosely over the lapel of
his coat. Since, with his back partly toward Dona Felisberta, he
blocked the girl, only afterwards, when he, in the involving way
he had of surrounding her, moved aside a little, could Dona
Felisberta see her. And it seemed to her as well, it barely seemed
to her, that she had seen the girl before. But she did not pursue
the matter, because she could not see clearly from that distance,
because she was not used to focusing her eyes in that way, and
because she began to hear a voice in her memory, snickering

beneath a moustache stroked with jesting petulance: "unhappy
Berta. . . ." In a reflex motion, she let go the curtain and, this
time with a conscious and prolonged complacency, scratched
herself behind one ear and, after this, above her forehead. Once
again she took the curtain in the fingers of her left hand and then
bent her body sideways toward the windowpane. Unobstructed
now by the boy and clearly facing Dona Felisberta, the girl
raised, toward what must have been an insidious voice, her big,
fascinated eyes that gleamed with the same blackness as her hair
parted in the middle, and that heaved like the breast hidden in a
green dress, from the shoulders of which her arms hung alongside her body. This Dona Felisberta did not notice, inept at
distinguishing details with the exception of whatever it was in
the girl's face that reminded her of the portrait of her grandmother who, however, did not have that rosy and yet dark air,
and who could not really have been compared to the slightly
awkward girl who was backing toward the wall of the building,
almost in a dawning flight, quite different from the pensive
languishing in the portrait and making it so apparent that no
one had ever languished in just that way. Dona Felisberta, who
had forgotten even what she was gazing at, in the rapture of
reconstituting the portrait that for so long she had not contemplated, was startled by the jangle of the doorbell. Annoyed, she
got up, placed on the small chair the old clothes she was working on, and went to the door. Through the grille a badly dressed
fellow asked her if Senhor Silva lived there, a Senhor Silva who
had moved from St. Lazaro Street. Dona Felisberta, in an impatience that was not like her, dryly insisted that she knew
nothing about any Silvas, that no one had moved there or
nearby. She returned to the window, and now unhurriedly
picked up the sewing and sat down, shifting the curtain in order to see. Totally unaware of the people passing on the other
street, slowly, or hurriedly and carrying their lunches in hand,
emerging from or disappearing into the framed vision of Dona

Felisberta who paid no attention to them and gazed, with a fixed
and fleeting look, at the couple, the boy held the girl against the
wall with his body which was curved over her and with his arm
that, supported by the wall from which she was nervously moving, impeded the motion of sliding toward the grocery store
which she was trying hesitantly to carry out. Dona Felisberta
looked without understanding, absorbed only in an attentive
contemplation to which, for the first time, she yielded. But
something in her throbbed in a glimmer of identification that
sharpened and diffused, in a subtle to-and-fro, in the empty
recesses of her spirit that had never been populated with images.
Rapidly bending his hips, the boy pressed the girl against the
wall, and backed away straightening up his body, once again
burying in his trouser pocket his left hand that had been spread
out on the wall next to the girl's head. She remained still,
somewhat irresolute, and, slowly, the boy took hold of her right
arm, as if dragging her with a faint gesture which his curved and
twitching fingers made compelling. They walked along as far as
the edge of the grocery store pavement and crossed to the opposite corner, where the girl stopped, and he, without releasing
her, took a step forward, keeping his back to the corner window
and the fixed and innocent eye of Dona Felisberta. Having
placed her chair so as not to face her nearest neighbors, Dona
Felisberta could not, without twisting around, follow their
movements, which suddenly became rapid, with the girl looking from side to side as if fearful of being seen. But what
astonished Dona Felisberta was the sweet and smiling glaze that
the girl's eyes superimposed on the expression of suspicion that
had been directed at the occasional passers-by. And they disappeared beyond the window, the boy walking, still holding the
girl, but without turning his head to her, as if he were carrying
with him an inanimate and mute object.

Dona Felisberta sat for some time, still holding the curtain, seeing only the opposite corner on whose reddened paint

she began to distinguish features, spots, designs, forms, that seemed to extend to the white paving of the walk, and which she had never noticed. In her tired eyes, unused to staring and to motives, those spots and forms took shape, then scattered in unhurried metamorphoses. She noticed a discomfort which, in a reflex itch that she scratched, she identified as a subtle ache in her raised arm. She let go the curtain, rested her eyes on her lap where her two hands already lay folded, and noticed how white and fine the hands were, her hands, pallidly emaciated atop the grimy sewing. She got up from the chair and went slowly to the sitting room, whose door she opened; and she turned on the light. The portrait of her grandmother was on the wall facing her, between the two closed windows. Dona Felisberta saw that the artist had not painted her hands, vague rosy shapes that were lost in the darkness which held only some shades of green from her dress. To verify that this was so, for it had never been a part, as knowledge, of the commentaries passed down in the family, she drew closer. And she had the sudden sensation of not being alone. Indeed, her own image, side by side with the image of her grandmother, was returned to her, duplicated in the mirror. She looked at them, and she looked at herself. In the mirror—and a long time had passed since she had last seen herself in a mirror, for she barely looked at herself in the dressing-table mirror on the rare occasions when she arranged some loose strands of hair which dirt and time kept in position during her calm and quiet sleeps—in the weak light of the ceiling chandelier, blurred even further by spiderwebs intertwined with the thick wires of the glass prisms hanging from a darkened metal crown; and beyond the cracks in the worn-out tin: in the mirror, yes, there was her image, or the image that used to be hers, for Dona Felisberta did not recognize it as such, in a comparison forced on her by the way her head seemed to lean against her grand-mother's, like a picture postcard. She took a few steps and sat down on the edge of one of the chairs, with her hands pressed together in her lap, her back straightened, as on those rare occasions in the old days when she would ceremoniously receive visitors there, treating herself with even more ceremony than she had ever displayed toward them. The room had some furniture, above all étagères of various sizes covered with little cups and saucers that had been, for the most part, wedding presents. And two armchairs made, like the sofa and the two chairs without arms, of a common and highly polished wood, with open flowers carved into the straight backs and seats upholstered in sham crimson velvet, which had been acquired by Henriques much later. It was said in the neighborhood (Dona Felisberta had learned from that maid) that the "other woman" had been given the same furniture. Dona Felisberta unconsciously retained a certain aversion to the furniture, even after the "other woman" had moved (simultaneously from the house opposite the sitting-room windows and from the other house set up by Henriques, already at that time carrying on with a wretched creature from Bairro Alto who wanted only the going rate and made no demands, according to what he told Dona Felisberta), and she had come to know (through the same maid whom she had dismissed after Henriques's death, as if she had been part, and in a sense she had, of all that was being buried with him) that the "other's" furniture was not at all similar, and was (to the maid's taste) much uglier. At that very spot she had sat for the last and almost first time, when she received the final visits, those of condolences, which she had never later repaid. And she had sat just like that, as she was suddenly reminded by the uncomfortable and rough gap between the loose upholstery and the frame of the seat, a gap unlike the soft and gradual curve of her little chair. A tentatively begun itch, which for her was no longer even an itch but merely a habit, something to fill her mind, irritated her unexpectedly. She did not scratch herself, although, in an instinctive gesture, she had actually raised her hand with fingers delicately bent and the little finger almost erect. And then she felt the desire to seat herself seriously in the chair. She drew herself up, resting her hands on the arms of the chair; she leaned back, keeping her curved hands where they rested; she breathed deeply. So she remained for a long time, thinking of nothing, with nothing crossing her imagination, not murmuring to herself, not feeling anything. Eyes half-closed, breathing calmly, Dona Felisberta drifted in a well-being that was neither sensation nor consciousness, until a sharp pain in the pit of her stomach reminded her that she was hungry. Dona Felisberta's hunger was relative, and would have been satisfied with the leftovers she had carefully set aside at lunch. She got up with eyes lowered, not seeing herself or the painting, turned off the light and left the room. But she had to return, to close the door that she had left open. And, although she knew automatically the height of the door handle, which was a knob made of porcelain with a yellow metal base, on every door in the house, she needed to grope for it because, as she then realized, night had fallen. From that point on, until she lay down and fell asleep, everything was as on other days.

In the morning, Dona Felisberta woke up early, as usual, and let herself lie in a sleepy lethargy, also as usual, not because the sun was entering the gloomy room to give her a foretaste of the clear summer morning, but simply because she had never had any reason for getting up promptly, and now had even less. Dona Felisberta's bedroom, now as throughout her married life, faced the back, and the high window overlooked a small veranda, on which the kitchen door also opened, which had a wooden partition in one corner with a small door on the other side of which, in malodorous darkness, was a kind of wooden bench with an oval hole, the only sanitary installation in the old house. The veranda looked onto a narrow yard, property of the ground floor; a high wall, with a grating covered and crowned by a vine grown leafy by its nature and by neglect, separated the yard and the street. Opposite the veranda, intercepted only by some narrow and scant slits corresponding to each floor, there arose the high wall of the neighboring building, scored by huge gaps in the whitewashed plaster whose fallen residue whitely stained the yellow earth of the yard where some scrawny plants flowered, but in cans and in broken vases dispersed at random under a net crisscrossed with enough slack wires to dry the clothing of a battalion, and from which there never hung more than a few pieces, white and forgotten, each far from the others. From the veranda, then, there was no view, and nothing could be seen of the street because of the vines and the distance at which the veranda ended from any alignment with the building's façade, which was the width of the dining room adjacent to Dona Felisberta's bedroom. The house was organized around a corridor that, as one entered, had on the right the sitting room door, at the rear the door of the corner room, and at the left, successively, the doors of the kitchen, bedroom, and dining room. Aside from the regular and almost mechanical visits to the cubicle on the veranda, the lengthy but almost immaterial preparations of food (rare, indeed, for days on end) at the coal stove which she fanned conscientiously in order to revive some economical embers whose ashes she almost never shook out, Dona Felisberta's life was in fact confined to the compartment at the corner and, from morning to night, to the immured bedroom whose furniture of dark and varnished wood made it even more gloomy. She never went into the dining room, for which she had no use, and kept in the kitchen those dirty utensils with which she ate, seated on the bench and contemplating, through the windows (one of which had broken and been repaired with a piece of paper), the wall opposite. On that morning, after getting up and lighting the fire and going to the door to retrieve the bag which every night she hung outside so that the breadman each day would leave a small loaf (the day after receiving her pension, Dona Felisberta would put enough money in the bag for a month of small loaves), she sat down to wait for the much reheated coffee to warm up—she kept it already prepared in large quantities in a big clay pitcher. And, as she waited, it seemed to her that the coffee was taking a long time to steam. She got up to fan the stove, some ashes soared. Once again she sat down. When at last the coffee steamed, she lifted the pot, poured some into a mug that contained at its bottom years of dregs drunk to the last drop, and could not find the bread that she had placed next to the mug. Troubled, puzzled, she looked around. Crumbs spread on the table proved, to her shock, that, absorbed, she had eaten the tiny loaf—the entire loaf!—meant to last the whole day. Dona Felisberta could not chide herself enough, could not imagine how such a thing had happened. But it was done. Sadly, she sipped the coffee in carefully spaced-out tiny gulps. She moved from the kitchen into the corridor and, when her eyes focused, found herself looking at the walk across from the dining room, holding in her hand curtains which were not those of the corner window. For the window was one of the two windows in the dining room, where she never entered, where she never thought of entering, but where she now was. Dona Felisberta took several steps into the room, stood next to the badly warped table, and fixed her eyes on a toothpick holder on top of the waxed sideboard whose doors were all roughly carved apples and pears. The toothpick holder, made of white metal, had belonged to her grandmother and represented, on a pedestal with four tiny gnarled feet, a slender figure, perhaps of a shepherd, half naked, supported by a staff that had long since disappeared, and carrying on his back a knapsack from which protruded the toothpicks. The movement of the little figure, with one hand at its waist and the other firmly leaning on something invisible, was of a strange, inexplicable swaying. Its head hung a little forward and, worn by constant cleaning with chalk in times gone by and now tarnished and speckled like the whole body, had acquired an expression that held Dona Felisberta though she in no sense took in this figure which, in fact, she did not know how to see. She went out of the dining room and, as she was about to enter the corner room, a terrible itch on the top of her head made her stop. She scratched herself angrily, trying to seize the louse, and was horrified at the idea of killing it between her nails. Returning to her bedroom, she rummaged through drawers, found innumerable things that she had forgotten and that intrigued her because they had been put safely away, and ended up discovering a fine comb. She put it to her hair, but it hurt her too much. She could not run it through her tangled and matted strands of hair. From the top of her dressing table she took a wide comb and combed what soon transformed itself into thin and bristly, vaguely wavy hair which, as she could see in the mirror, framed a wrinkled face with baggy eyes, with craws of thin skin hanging from the seams of her lips, accompanying the collapse of her cheeks. She looked at that image fascinated. Her eyes, following the details of her face, were shining, and she saw them looking back at her symmetrically askance. Her lips tapered off, their corners hiding in her fallen jowls. Dona Felisberta did not manage to note that she was smiling, for a sudden itch made her concentrate once again on the combs, using first one, then the other, persistently and, for all she knew, enthusiastically.

The rest of the day passed in comparable confusion, with Dona Felisberta finding herself in the most unforeseeable places, noticing a bad odor in the potatoes cooked with a slice of smoked sausage, and even tripping on a crack in the floor of the corridor which she had avoided for years merely by ignoring it. Only late in the afternoon, a calm took hold of Dona Felisberta as she sat in her small chair whose position, seeming to her inconvenient for leaning back, she had repeatedly changed, in the end turning it around the better to command the corner opposite, where the young couple had stopped before continuing up the street. And the curtain knew no rest, even when

Dona Felisberta was finally allayed as, unexpectedly given her unconscious appetites and gestures, the boy at last appeared, but all alone, walking down the block by the grocery store and stopping at the corner. Dona Felisberta then watched him closely, with the same ambiguous distraction that she had brought to her contemplation of the toothpick holder. He was dressed as before, this Dona Felisberta noted. And he swayed, hands in pockets, a rhythmic motion to his slender body whose long legs took short expectant steps, with an occasional kick at a box of matches or an orange peel fallen to the ground. Dona Felisberta took this in, but did not notice it, just as she took in his thin face, his nose, and the ears that seemed detached from his head, to which his mop of hair, undecided in both its color and its way of falling forward, also seemed a stranger. His thick lips, wide mouth, sharp chin and prominent cheekbones, his deep-set, large, and darkened eyes and his sideways and lowered glance darting from beneath strong ridges arched like a second set of brows, all this Dona Felisberta visually digested, growing slightly irritated when he, in his brief wandering, turned his back to her and moved in the direction of the barricade, letting his gaze linger once as he stopped at the edge of the spot where he had held the girl against the wall. But quickly her irritation changed to gratified contemplation, for it was now his back that she saw, the curve of his buttocks, and the slight bent of some-one who does not straighten his knees completely, apparent in the uncertain slackening of his otherwise tight trousers. But Dona Felisberta was not thinking of the minutiae of these obser-vations. Oddly, she thought instead of the toothpick holder, brought to her mind by the dim metallic sheen that, in her eyes, the figure of the boy seemed to emit. That time was passing, neither the dusk nor the din of swinging doors disclosed to Dona Felisberta, but rather a pained impatience that she felt, commu-nicated through the tedium of waiting, through the annoyance of his deluded control and betrayed desire, through a glimmer of tender and anxious concern, evident in the boy's movements. It was almost night when he, after glancing toward several streets, decided to give up and, in an angry impulse, crossed the street. Hurriedly, in rapid jolts that cut off her breathing, Dona Felisberta got up, left the room, entered the dining room and went to the first window and then the second to accompany with her eyes the progression of the boy who, slowly now and with backward glances, continued down the sidewalk. Disconsolate, Dona Felisberta stood immobile behind the second window, even long after the figure of the boy was out of sight. She was not disconsolate for having waited in vain for a meeting, nor for having been deprived of a meeting, nor even because the figure which was so detailed in her eyes had disappeared, out of reach of the indecision of that dirty and defective glass which was the very transparency of life as she saw it. It was not this, but a distress far beyond herself, beyond even the identification with someone waiting or someone being awaited. Dona Felisberta returned to the corner window and sat in the low chair, penetrating little by little into gloomy, dripping, and freezing vaults from which hung, like mended old clothes suspended on laundry lines, fragments of memories, phrases, a shoulder, a finger, the color of a dress, a table leg, the outline of a key, an open book whose pages were turning, a window with a grating and light entering, receipts, crumbs on the red-and-white checkered oilcloth, a coin clinking and then rolling down the corridor, a procession of things and of gestures retreating behind her one after another in a calm flow. And yet it seemed to Dona Felisberta that, at heart, here was a clarity that was not illusion, and she felt pity, genuine pity, for a figure that she saw outlined and twisting in space. It was a very young girl, of average height and slim waist, with long and shapely legs, broad hips, pointed breasts that nonetheless gently formed a rounded bosom, an oval face bordered by black hair parted in the middle, almond eyes, a very small upturned nose, and a heavy and compact mouth that contracted in worried uncertainty. Dona Felisberta wasn't sure how, against the light, she could distinguish her so clearly. And when she saw her illuminated by the lamp on the corner, motionless at the edge of the pavement, haloed by the light that fell upon her, then she recognized her. In a flash, Dona Felisberta, petrified with anguish in the chair, mentally told her that he had been there, had stopped at the corner and then continued down the street. He had not abandoned her, had not forgotten her, nor had anything happened to him to make him miss their meeting. But the girl did not hear, and a small itch in her temple made Dona Felisberta return to herself. The girl retreated further toward the wall of the building, took a few steps in the direction in which the boy had led her, stopped, turned back to the corner. Dona Felisberta's hands shook, she pricked her finger with the sewing needle. The curtain, so used to the ordinary gesture that lifted it aside, revealed that the girl was leaving, no, she was turning back, no, she was leaving, no, she was going down the street, no, she was stopping, was going to turn back, no no, she was drawing close to the wall, yes, she had leaned against it, no, she was going to the edge of the pavement as if to cross the street toward the grocery corner. A car passed in front of her. And suddenly the boy was behind her, grasping her by the shoulders and leaning his head close to her neck and to her hair which, in the fright that shook her, tremulously covered his shoulders. Dona Felisberta, also trembling, stood up, letting her sewing fall. And she felt a warmth running down her cheeks. In her usual gesture, with her finger semi-erect, she raised her hand and brought it to her face. The hand felt wet. Wet? Yes, wet, because she was crying. But crying why? she asked herself. And, once again, she looked outside. They had crossed the street, were going by the grocery corner, heading for the barricade. On her feet, next to the window, Dona Felisberta did not need to lift the curtain aside, for she could see above it. The light of the streetlamps, fragmented by the defects in the windowpane, dazed her, but, shifting her head to coordinate the movements of the two with the reflections that lengthened and retracted, she could see them now stop close to the spot where they had been and, immediately thereafter, in a clatter of confused steps during which the boy's arms grasped by the waist the girl who, melting, wrapped one arm across his back, they moved to the darkened doorway of one of the buildings. With one arm he continued pressing against him the girl whose hands could be seen on his shoulders, while with the other arm he pushed at the door which would not open. His arm persisted and then joined the other arm, entwining the girl in a violence that wavered like his head, swaying from side to side as he pressed his mouth against her face, which was hidden. And their two bodies formed one confused mass that, wavering, hinted at slowly moving hips from which, moments later, the girl seemed to hang on the points of her toes, as the boy's legs bent in a continuous tremor. Dona Felisberta, leaning against the window molding, eyes wide open, was in a cold sweat. And then, whether by mere chance or finally giving way, the door opened and the two almost fell into the building in a shuddering thud that suffocated Dona Felisberta. But immediately thereafter, she saw that the door was closing.

Dona Felisberta squeezed shut her eyes in which little lights danced, growing into perpetual circles of other lights that opened from still others. Her head sagged and her body slid along the window molding in a complete slackening of her joints. She sat down unaware in the chair and let her head fall forward. Over her whole body there passed a slight trembling which eventually settled in her knees. And she felt nothing more except for a pearly string of chilled sweat which did not run but was like an early morning dew condensing on her. Some of the lice that had escaped her fine comb tickled her, but she did not notice. As she raised her head with a sigh, her hand mechanically but hesitantly turned the curtain back in a broad gesture. The door was wide open. No one could be seen. Then Dona Felisberta heard a laugh, a high, penetrating, joyful laugh, amused, tender, anxious, and calm, that grew and made her jaw ache. And, in a kind of luminous and flashing roar, Dona Felisberta laughed.

From that day on her life changed completely. With an enormous effort, painfully humiliated, constantly sensing that something was amiss, Dona Felisberta picked her lice, washed herself, washed her clothes, cleaned the house; or, rather, tried to pick her lice and wash herself. She hunted down bugs, swept all the rooms, shook all the cobwebs she could reach with her raised broom grown bare and bent from its long sleep against the back of the kitchen door. Daily, her struggle continued in a constant effort from which Dona Felisberta only rested, exhausted and happy, late in the afternoon, in her chair by the window, there to follow with laughing eyes the couple's maneuvers. They had not returned to that spot but met regularly at the grocery store corner and, after a more or less lengthy conversation, would continue on down the street. Dona Felisberta would then go to observe them from the windows of the dining room, moving on to the kitchen where, in china that she now courageously scoured, she ate the same insignificant things as always, but in unheard of combinations of foods and relative proportions, which she tried out, and with sophisticated seasonings lamentably mutilated by lack of habit arrived at from her never very secure knowledge. And the days passed. Dona Felisberta made great changes in her sewing, eliminating innumerable rags from her drawers, and restoring with the most serviceable pieces the little clothing that she owned. She even struggled with a problem the solution of which she had long since forgotten—where to put the garbage that was accumulating in the corner of the veranda, for she lacked the courage to place it little by little, at night, in the garden below, as had occurred to her after one

housecleaning. She long hesitated to put a small bundle in the
doorway, which was what she had ordered done in the old days.
But she could see, in the doorways of the other buildings, some
identical pails that, she now remembered having heard in the
grocery store, were obligatory. Laboriously, she made packets
and bundles that remained piled up in the corner of the veranda.
And one night, having witnessed the most loving, tender gestures enveloped by the most softly murmured words, Dona
Felisberta resolved to go out and to leave, along the doorways,
two or three burdensome bundles, which, after many glances to
one side and the other, she deposited several blocks away, returning hurriedly while they in their whiteness pursued her
accusingly from the thresholds on which they had been placed.
There were days when the young couple did not appear for their
meeting at dusk. These were Sundays or the most official holidays, for then the grocery store would not open and greater calm
descended on the street. By mere chance, as she orbited in her
now interminable and nearly possessed cleaning—for dirt so
slowly accumulated and serenely encrusted did not rapidly surrender to her solitary efforts, devoid of strength and method—
Dona Felisberta discovered that, if they appeared on those days,
it was much earlier and with the look of people preparing for an
outing in the country or at the beach. Dona Felisberta watched,
smiling softly, how one of them would wait for the other, at
times with a large bag in hand from which the necks of several
bottles protruded. And, when the other would arrive, the two
would hurry off, like people running to catch a bus. Dona
Felisberta did not mentally inquire, not even in the illusions to
which she continued to abandon herself, what their lives might
be like, where they came from, with whom they lived, why they
didn't live together, why they used to meet there, what they
lived on, where they were going, nothing. It was as if they had
no secrets from her, as if she lived, in each one, like a silent
witness of something she need not know at each moment, for
the sequence of moments was her participation in those lives.

At times, many times, busy with her cleaning, with the restoration of her wardrobe, with the precarious perfecting of a presence she had never had, Dona Felisberta would forget to eat. She would not have been able to say, had she thought to ask herself, if she had eaten lunch or dinner, if she had had her coffee that morning. One or another time she had gone out to buy some small item at the grocery store, where she was waited on by the owner, his brow furrowed in surprise, much to her embarrassment. More than once she had needed to buy coal, she, who used to buy it from the coal merchant on the block in tiny amounts that lasted for weeks. And one day, the clanging of the doorbell awakened her at her post, in the small low chair, when such a sound had been almost effaced from her memory, for, by coincidence, misinformed people had to all appearances ceased to imagine that the Silvas who had moved from St. Lazaro Street lived there. Through the grille, as she was saying that it was the wrong house, if only because an untimely apparition had interrupted the absorption in which she sat suspended, she saw a bald fellow with a cigarette in the corner of his mouth, who rang again as she, having closed the grille, was retreating down the corridor. Dona Felisberta felt a kind of anger, troubled by a suspicious uneasiness, and through the grille she heard the fellow's lips say: "I came to see how you are," and even before she recognized him she was in a panic, unable to guess how long it had been since she had last received a visit or gone to pay the rent. She opened the door and the two looked at one another with fleeting and perplexed eyes. Dona Felisberta stammered: "I've been busy cleaning the house . . ." and he repeated, "I didn't know what happened to you. . . . I even thought. . . ." And she interrupted: "Everything was so dirty! . . ." The man cleared his throat, grabbed the tip of the cigarette almost with his yellowed nails and, straightening somewhat his pot-bellied bulk, asked: "Have you forgotten? Is that it? . . ." but rapidly sank back into his flabbiness, saying, "I came to see how you are. . . ." "Oh, I'm well, very well, thank you." Dona

Felisberta's panic had strangely dissolved, had lost its importance. It was as if none of that had anything to do with her life,
with that very house she was cleaning. She was not trying to
change the subject by insisting on what was occupying her, but,
making an effort in the face of the man's indecision—he stood
there still, beginning to take on the shape of an empty little
chair with a sunken cane seat—she said: "I forgot, it's just that I
forgot." And he, unable to find words with which to speak to
the ghost of a creature he had supposed dead and buried and who
now appeared to him with such calm indifference, persisted:
"Well, if you forgot. . . . Fine, you forgot. . . . And now . . .
what shall we do? All this time! . . ." "Time?" Dona Felisberta
repeated, and the question hung in the air between the two of
them, in the diffused brightness of the landing. "Then you'll go
there, won't you?" he finally asked. "Yes, I can go. . . . Ah . . .
would you like to come in?" "No, thank you. I've brought the
receipts. . . ." "You've gone out of your way, let me see . . .
but come in, please. . . ." "Thank you, but here they are. . . .
Then you'll go there, won't you?" "I'll go, I'll get the money
and go . . ." and Dona Felisberta flushed slightly as she added:
"I've forgotten to get it. . . ." "You forgot . . . but you'll go,
won't you?" And Dona Felisberta, gazing vaguely at the receipts
in her hand, did not answer. The man stood there, shifting
slightly from one foot to the other. Then he placed his fingers on
the banister of the staircase, turned to descend, looked once
more at her, and began his descent. At the bottom he stopped
on the landing and, before proceeding heavily down the next
flight, raised his head to say: "Then you'll go there, won't
you? . . ." and, going down the steps, disappeared. Dona Felisberta closed the door, searched hesitantly for a place to set the
receipts, forgot them, and went to sit in her small chair. They
must be about to arrive, who would come first? She had been
spending her savings. Would they converse? Savings? Would
they be late? What would she do now with the pension? Would

they leave right away? She had to go out, to find out what she must do. Which way would they walk? Perhaps they would no longer pay her. Would she be wearing the green dress? . . . And Dona Felisberta looked at the door they had entered, and which now seemed impossible to close, always half open, more or less ajar, more at the mercy of its jammed hinges. Conjectures crisscrossed and then effaced one another, the appearance of some seemed to authorize that of others which then used this authorization to suppress them. A hint of a smile appeared on Dona Felisberta's lips, a smile of confidence, of certainty, perhaps even of hope. And a dusty reflection of the sun's lights, an orange-colored and suspended brightness that permeated the crossroads, left on her hair a silky whiteness, a serenely transparent wave, and gave to her head a majestic bearing, completed in paradoxical dignity by the sharp collarbone protruding from her bodice and by her fallen and withered breast.

Dona Felisberta continued to wait, occasionally following with her intense gaze the people who passed by, but following them only as mere pauses in her anticipation. If she had never before been interested in acknowledging them, if their passage had never penetrated her distant and fleeting interest, less than ever, now, could these "others" hold her. Her whole being was the concealed, patient, complicitous witness to that amorous union, with neither words nor gestures; the invisible guardian of a silence in which their image proceeded to dance a dance whose meaning was, or appeared to be, outside of that exclusive world to which they all belonged, actors and spectator. At that moment Dona Felisberta felt that something was happening within her. It was like a piercing, an excision, a detaching of something very intimate, physical, carnal. She looked outside. They weren't at the grocery store corner but at the corner opposite. She, leaning against the wall, was speaking animatedly, waving her hands in a way unusual for her; and he, with one shoulder also leaning against the wall, his hands in the pockets of his trousers and one foot crossed over the other, was listening, or, rather, was manifestly not listening. At last she grew quiet, joined her two hands and let her arms fall; and, without changing their positions, thus they both remained for some time. She then raised one of her hands and rested it on the boy's arm. He uncrossed his feet, straightened up from the wall, took a few steps around her, which blocked Dona Felisberta's view of him and made the girl's hand slide down, drop, and, returning to her earlier position, join her other hand which could not be seen. Without looking closely at her, and even casting to one side and the other his oblique glance which would have emerged from those protruding and curved brows, he spoke, undoubtedly in a slow manner, with frequent pauses. To Dona Felisberta's sensation of piercing, excision, and detachment there was now added a chill, a cutting and harsh breeze, at once balmy in its implacable and frozen movement and disturbing and dominating, at once a contradictory pleasure and a horror, a violence, a violation, a. . . . Dona Felisberta got to her feet at the precise moment that, terrified and defeated, she was about to hear, through years of memory, the voice saying: "unhappy Berta. . . ." But she did not hear it, for in a brusque gesture, struggling against the latch that stubbornly resisted, she flung the window open, leaned out, waved her arms, and must have prevailed over the clatter of the window opening, with an inarticulate, howling, and rasping roar, a splendid cry, an offering of herself and of her house, so that love, if it was love, would not be lost.

They both raised their eyes to the corner window, and Dona Felisberta saw their faces, mouths open, disturbed, puzzled, pained, half-scoffing, suspicious, shamed by the invisibility of months betrayed in one second. Alike before Dona Felisberta's agitation, frozen now into a cheerful and inviting intimacy, something united them—an invincible youthfulness, completely innocent and abandoned, purely virginal, tranquilly indecent and gay, avidly dedicated to possessing and pleasuring itself. But this very thing soon separated them. Dona Felisberta, in a daze, felt—as she had never before felt—a fecundity spreading through her, a rounding of her belly, and she felt herself give birth, and that her children's children played on her knees. They, meanwhile, hastily, in a haste that slowed into lightly lingering pauses drawing them further apart, had separated, she disappearing below the window, in an unusual direction that concealed her; he continuing, without longing or desire, in the direction in which he had so many times taken her, turning his back to the blind alley where a door would no longer close.

Dona Felisberta tripped on the crack in the corridor, slipped on the landing of the ground floor on a peel that had fallen there, and was further constrained by her traditional fear of passing the neighbors' door. She stood hesitantly on the sidewalk, not knowing which way to turn. But she did know. Suddenly, she turned the corner and went up the street, out of breath, in tiny, vacillating, and hurried steps, and, in the middle of the long block, she crossed the street diagonally, hearing close to her a stentorian stridency and a shouting that she soon left behind. At the end, she stopped and looked. She rounded the corner and continued at what was, for her, a run. The face that, bent down, was staring at her obliquely, thin, with the nose shiny at its tip, the transparent ears, the thick and colorless lips, the hollow almost beardless cheeks, the chin further sharpened by a sparse and badly shaved beard, the hair fallen over one of the eyes that stared at her from a clouded and blue depth—this face was not open-mouthed, nor disturbed, nor puzzled, nor pained, nor half-scoffing, nor restless, nor was there any shame in the insistence with which he looked at her. Dona Felisberta opened her mouth to speak, closed it again, moved her lips, and heard an indistinct, far off, guttural voice say: "I've been busy cleaning the house. . . ." The boy's eyes blinked, hid themselves piercingly in his half-closed lids, and

his body slumped over one leg with a movement of his hips
elastically adjusting themselves. Dona Felisberta felt neither
disturbed nor confused but merely a chill that communicated an
extreme weariness to her, trembling through her legs and in the
hands that, raising them slightly, she contemplated. The chill
was increasing and made her take a few steps in the direction of
the corner she had rounded. She walked along, stopping before
rounding it again, and saw that the boy was turning back and
staring at her with the same piercing and still gaze. She rapidly
turned the corner and came down the street, glancing backward
from time to time. She saw then that the boy had also turned the
corner and was coming along the sidewalk with that swaying
and undulating gait, his back and belly curved, which seemed
to Dona Felisberta, in a pungent terror that chilled her once and
for all, to push her and make her run, literally run, toward her
own corner. Only once behind her door, which she closed with
her body, did she stop, while in her ears a clatter of feet, shouts,
creaking steps, doors opening and closing, convinced her that
the absolute silence of the dusk invading the building's staircase
was something more than the solitude filled by a monstrous
ticktock, surely not within her but echoing down in the depths
of the corridor, there where the brightness of the corner room
was outlined.

Drawn to the mournful bitterness which she distinctly saw
that fleeting brightness to be, Dona Felisberta moved along, in
a staggering and swaying gait, and stopped in front of the wide-
open window. Outlined in the reddish light that left blotches on
him, leaning against the opposite corner with his hands in his
trouser pockets, the boy had raised one foot, the left, propped it
on the wall, and stood looking at her insistently. Dona Felisberta, in contained, sibilant, short gasps, noted that terror and
disappointment were pouring out of her, closing the windows,
and setting her down carefully, tenderly, in the chair. The boy,
blinking his half-closed eyes, let his foot drop, straightened his

buttocks up from the wall, and plunged his hands more deeply into his pockets, like someone stretching his limbs. Then, secretively, his hands stirred, withdrew from his pockets now and then, and began to stir again, in an effort to establish both himself and his availability. Until, taking his hands from his pockets, he managed to fix on the figure behind the curtains a condescending and sarcastic gaze that now moved down his body and now stared again at the dimly glimpsed figure.

But Dona Felisberta's head had already slumped forward. And when, some time later, the doorbell sounded with a rapid and cautious touch, no movement escaped her. Merely, in the near total darkness into which the streetlamps suddenly released flashes of light that the windowpanes multiplied, some rather persistent lice decided at long last to abandon her.

1950–1960                    *Translated by Daphne Patai*

# The Commemoration

The valiant never taste of death
but once.
    *Shakespeare*, Julius Caesar

## I

*T*HE idea had sprung up in a café conversation, but the commanding voice of Gustavo Dores soon developed it to such a point that not even his habitual companions, swayed by the imperious emotion of the department head, dared claim the title of founding partners of the important commemoration they were to celebrate. It may seem strange that such an act of self-denial was made for the sake of a man incapable of acknowledging the value of any simple adventure befalling another and recounted there at the café whose tables for decades on end had suffered sketches of rivers, native villages, and positions for confronting the innumerable wild animals of the African hinterland. With the exception of Gustavo Dores and three or four of his "colleagues in the Ministry" (and these not very frequent due to the cool indifference with which outsiders from the continent were received except when they listened respectfully), all were retired civil servants, employees of the Treasury, or administrators who, though they longed for their old space and power and were fed up with the "secretariat" which had provided them with their real and imaginary experiences, still cautiously admired the bureaucracy in the Metropolis* which had formerly, in part, managed them, and now, also in part, maintained them. It was not, therefore, so surprising that they yielded to Gustavo Dores, for he combined, with his carefully meted out humility, the prestige owing to a man who had left the other side of the counter at the government office on the Terreiro do Paço and still sat with them, in their midst, out of a love for territories measured, in his mind, on stacks of books and folios. Moreover, on all this was imposed and superimposed, full of possibilities and implied influences, the officiating department head's persuasive voice reviving in them that tepid and ancient spirit of anonymous participation, and concentrating, in their customary corner of the café, that atmosphere of secret piety enhanced by the columns of false marble, the dark carved wood and the glazed tiles (embellished with detailed and ugly historical scenes suited to the whims of the middle class), and borne by the tremulos of the quartet, very proficient in the "Portuguese Rhapsody," which always ended in a long and solemn crescendo amidst the gooseflesh of the habitués and a few bars of the national anthem.

In less than a month it would be the tenth anniversary of the obscure death of João Pereira Castanheira who, from a wretched clerk working at the counter of a general store in the hinterland, had risen to become a respected trader in Africa, defended Namucala against the rebellious heathen, guided expeditionary forces of the Occupation, governed a province (there had been a controversy over whether it was, at that time, a province or a district), and had ended his days in Lisbon, perhaps striken by biliousness ("the doctors in the Metropolis are never competent when it comes to tropical diseases"), and without ever getting used to the streetcars for which he had acquired a pass "so as to be able to get off the wrong ones without

---

* Metropolitan Portugal, as opposed to its colonies known euphemistically as overseas "territories" or "provinces" (Ed.).

constantly shelling out coins." It was precisely in connection with the defense of Namucala, whose "strategy" they had been debating heatedly, that the idea of the commemoration had taken form. To remember that man, brandishing his white beard in Lisbon and never receiving any special attention, who, though one of them, had reached a position there that they had been unable to attain for one or another reason—if not the arbitrariness of a superior, then the intrigue of a peer or the accusations of an inferior (there was always someone to be blamed, and stories were then told about bribes honestly rejected); it was to remember the past, as it was or might have been, of a class, "his" class ("yours," Gustavo Dores emphasized with simplicity); it was to call to public attention "by means of a modest but significant act, a life of dangers and responsibilities," and all had admired Castanheira, who had always hoisted in the bosom of the group of habitués the envied banner of the independent merchant confronting the bureaucracy. And, besides, the fellow had a good sense of humor! They had all gleefully admired that trick played on Rebelo, a poor fellow who was married and head of a border post. Whenever Castanheira wanted to get his people across the border, he would invite the Rebelos. Everybody would get through and for each one Castanheira had the horn of an African buffalo placed in Rebelo's house. Poor Rebelo was worried, even sick, over those horns which were filling up the house, not knowing where they were coming from, for all his servants had been well paid off. And the horns, which gradually became more numerous and soon covered everything, began to appear in Rebelo's own bedroom. Tormented, Rebelo went so far as to separate from his wife, who later lived with a sergeant until he abandoned her in Luanda when he returned to the Metropolis. It was only long afterwards that Rebelo, in Luanda to present himself before the Junta, learned the truth of the story and forgave his wife whom he found, so he now judged, to be a very serious and lonely woman.

With the fundamentals of the commemoration agreed

upon, Gustavo Dores worked untiringly on the project. He
knew Matos, an editor of the *Business Daily,* for whom he had
acted as intermediary in a matter of obtaining loans for bureaucrats, and through him he arranged for the publication of
a "simple announcement" which appeared twice, "in the obituaries too, for those who only read the obituaries." Other
newspapers followed suit; Dores spoke to many people in the
Ministry; it was rumored that the minister himself, in a conversation with the director-general, had praised the project. At the
office, the chief, behind his glasses with dark, thick frames
which convey solemnity and command respect, devoted every
spare moment to the commemoration; all the clerks avoided
interrupting him when they saw him bent over his desk constantly changing his pen and certainly drafting another news
item or taking notes for what he would say to Mr. So-and-So.
Besides, it was said of Gustavo Dores that the calmness with
which he gave a rebuttal and his unfailingly opportune observa-
tions were due to precisely this persistence. He read many newspapers and magazines and would immediately cite an identical
case that had occurred in Persia or in Poland; international
politics were like a lived experience to him. His sympathies,
however, which would oscillate somewhat according to the for-
tunes revealed by the war communiqués, were always in the end
encouraged by the hope for a victory—by whom and for what
reason he really didn't know. Indeed, when some of the minor
bureaucrats were inclined to favor the totalitarian countries,
carried away by a nostalgia for their own importance and by
their haughty contempt for Negroes—"to be Negro is to be a
servant"—he felt a certain administrative bliss; but when that
contempt, putting on aristocratic airs, was extended to the
colonists "who had arrived carrying all their possessions on their
backs," Gustavo Dores, though he limited himself to a handy
mimicry of a vague acquiescence, did not partake of their views
and even ventured, on one occasion, the opinion that Cas-

tanheira had begun by being more or less that very thing. Immediately the conversation had quickened; once more there poured forth events and surprising incidents: Castanheira had not walked with a hoe on his shoulder; and Gustavo Dores had merely revived his "untimely passion," as Medeiros, the head of another department, had sneered, to which Passos Silva, who belonged to Dores's department and in spite of detesting him, had responded: "patriotism is no respecter of age"—a rejoinder acclaimed with applause and laughter throughout the Ministry, until it finally reached the ears of Gustavo Dores from the mouth of the messenger Januário, his personal informant. Gustavo Dores smiled at the criticism and the reply in the same spirit with which he had coldly rejected Pereira Cláudio, another department head, who had become too interested in the commemoration and had tried to involve himself in it.

## II

At last the day arrived. The ceremony had been set for ten in the morning, an hour that ultimately suited only Gustavo Dores's punctuality, since the others either had nothing to do or were starting work at around that time. Even delaying it until Sunday had been considered, but Dores had demonstrated the inconvenience which that change would cause "for those who take no further notice of what they have once read," and he had made clear "the bad effect, which all knew from personal experience, of postponing any ceremony, no matter how postponable it might be. Was this one postponable? No, it was not."

The evening before, Dores had repeatedly told Dona Conceição to wake him one hour earlier. Dona Conceição had known about it, ever since "the commemoration had begun," but, as with other matters that she considered marginal to her own life, she had not responded in any way. They got along very well, they had an eighteen-year-old daughter who sang on Fridays at a private broadcasting station. Of course the station, too, had announced the commemoration and had even pledged to report on the event itself. Gustavo Dores alluded in the café to the "uncommon intelligence of those people, always ready to nourish an undertaking as well as to recognize talent."

From the bathroom, Gustavo Dores shouted: "And the flowers, have the flowers arrived?" They would take the flowers and silently place the bouquets, there would be no speeches. "So, have the flowers arrived or not? Hasn't Cristina returned yet?" She wouldn't be long, replied Dona Conceição. She wouldn't be long! . . . As if she were ever on time! . . . He would say some words, that would be expected: he had been the sponsor, the organizer, if they were there it was owing to him. A few simple words explaining the motive, with a passing reference to his efforts, and perhaps an anecdote about the deceased might not be a bad idea: comments of that type on such occasions are always touching and help sharpen memories. He left the bathroom and began to dress. If only those invited would show up. The items in the papers would have caught the attention of other people who would take advantage of the opportunity to renew old friendships. The radio was a great vehicle for informing people. There are those who don't read the paper and only hear news on the radio. Might they have heard Mimi? Would they have liked her? Certainly they liked her, she was a good singer. But the piano at the station was badly out of tune. He had never been able to buy a piano. Anyway, neither mother nor daughter knew how to play. If it were not for Dona Clotilde, the little one would not have had a place to practice her songs. A good lady, Dona Clotilde. "Oh, Conceição, where's my black tie? Things are never where they're supposed to be!" Under the handkerchiefs. Could it be there? It was impossible to get a proper knot in the black tie. It always ended up twisted. Let's see. That's not bad. That's it. Looping it twice. Already nine-thirty. And he still hadn't gotten the tie right. There, at last. "Conceição, I haven't heard Cristina come in yet." Of course, she still hadn't come. It would be better to buy the flowers on the way, anywhere. And now to change everything, that wasn't the right suit, it should have been the black one! But now there wasn't time, and anyway, to spend the rest of the day dressed in black! . . . At least it fitted well, that was something. Are you in mourning? No, I went to pay homage to Castanheira. "Conceição, where's the black waistcoat? Why didn't you lay everything out for me?" It isn't here. Ah, there it is. "Come and fasten the waistcoat. Good God, don't tighten it so much! What do you mean, you didn't realize! You do it on purpose. Whenever you see me so enthusiastic about something, happy. . . ." Happy, no; that wasn't appropriate for homage to a dead man. And why not? The joy of a duty carried out. Castanheira. He remembered Castanheira, very tall, with a white beard, his collar always loosened behind his beard. No. He remembered him, but seated at the table in the café with his hands resting on the top of his cane shaped into a dog's head, made of silver with eyes of red glass. His keys were missing, he had forgotten to transfer his keys. Now only the flowers. "Oh, Conceição, when Cristina comes, put the flowers wherever you wish. I'll buy some others on the way. Aren't I going to eat? So I'm not to have anything to eat!?"

He sat down at the table and, while eating the steak and rice left over from the night before, looked through the paper, examining the columns one by one. Perhaps in the obituaries. He looked again. Matos had forgotten. Or, rather, he had forgotten to remind Matos again. It would make no difference. Everybody knew. Those who found out at the last minute had an excuse for not appearing. There are always some who hear about things at the last minute.

"We need butter. Don't forget to get the butter downtown," Dona Conceição told him.

"Oh, I have so much on my mind, dear, today's such an important day, and you tell me not to forget the butter!"

Well, it's about time the flowers got here! It was ten

minutes to ten. He was going to arrive late. And if the streetcar were delayed, all of them would already be there. They would be waiting for him, certainly they would wait. And if he couldn't find the grave? He would, he had studied the place well. "See you later."

Gustavo Dores impatiently awaited the streetcar for Alto de São João. When one appeared, he eyed it carefully; perhaps someone on it would be going to the cemetery. Perhaps that man dressed in black. The man turned around and looked so curiously at the bouquet Gustavo Dores was carrying that he was about to ask him if he was also going to pay homage. As if he had divined the query, the man turned back and settled into his seat.

It was a beautiful morning, an immense crowd was in the street. But that street was always like that. It seemed like a fair. And the houses? Each one teemed with dozens of people, hanging from the verandas as if they couldn't fit inside.

A modest funeral, accompanied by people on foot, moved out of the way to let the streetcar pass. Would the men pulling the cart call themselves pallbearers? He had not gone to Castanheira's funeral. Why? Castanheira had disappeared, only afterwards was it learned that he had died. He had no family, not even in the provinces. He must have come from very humble origins. An apprentice store clerk. An apprentice store clerk fifty years ago in Africa! More than fifty years, certainly.

He got off at the square in front of the cemetery. Five past ten. He was almost on time. The man dressed in black had also gotten off and was entering the cemetery at a slow pace. Gustavo Dores, pretending to read an inscription while observing him out of the corner of his eye, let him pass ahead. He rearranged the bouquet of flowers. The man was walking very slowly, like someone heading nowhere in particular. He's not going, otherwise, he too would be in a hurry. Gustavo Dores quickened his pace and passed him by. The man looked at him again. Could he know me from someplace? He's a person who has nothing to do. What an idea: to come to the cemetery for a morning stroll! He was a . . . what do you call them? . . . a necrophiliac. Once he had read some story or other that had even taken place there in Alto de São João. In what book was it? He turned around. He couldn't see the man, who had entered some lane or other.

Two women dressed in black were coming up the road. They were talking. One of them was laughing. Such inappropriate behavior for a cemetery. Laughing at those lying here. He felt a great tenderness for his wife who would never again laugh after he died. It was still a long way to Castanheira's grave. He hadn't made a mistake, had he? No. A broken urn with bones peeping out, then the tomb with columns above the door. He was going the right way. It was a pleasant morning, a breeze was blowing and throughout the cemetery there was a great stillness. On Sundays some people bring bags with food. Now he saw the section behind which Castanheira lay. The others would be waiting for him around the trader's grave, all of them dressed in black, holding flowers and conversing in low voices. The stream of tombs concealed the scene; Gustavo Dores stiffened and rid his face of the good-natured expression that the fresh morning air had brought to it. He turned the corner. The graves continued down the slope; some people, here and there, were moving along within the apparently insurmountable network of railings, crosses, and more or less discolored tin boxes. No groups were in sight. Gustavo Dores looked around, still in disbelief, and then stood staring at the yellowish earth which, with the bouquets of withered flowers, resembled an immense garden devastated by the scattering of old iron; such a confused mass that the luxuriant flowering plants could not clearly emerge. This was the spot; there was no doubt about that, but nobody was there. Nobody had come. It was after ten past ten. Could his watch be fast?

He had set it the night before, by the pendulum clock! Nobody. The fault was his, he hadn't asked Matos to print it again on that very day. Most of them thought that the commemoration would not take place. Lots of people use such pretexts as an excuse, in order to convince themselves that it isn't worth the bother, that no one's going. And "someone" had come. If he, the sponsor, had not turned up, dozens of people would surely be there. It's always that way. People have no feelings, no conscience, nothing. They make promises and then fail to keep them. And they make their promises knowing full well they won't keep them, that they have no wish to go. Nobody has a sense of dignity: you think about paying homage to someone who represents the best of each of us, and it's as if, in each of us,there's not a thing of any use. But the greatest disrespect was not for the dead man who, poor guy, couldn't have cared less; the greatest disrespect was for him, the one who had worked so hard, who had organized it, and who had built up his own enthusiasm and that of the others. Yes, Castanheira didn't even suffer for all that; and who was suffering on account of Castanheira? He, the one who embodied the tribute to the great man. Poor Castanheira. So many years, so much effort, so much greatness, and everyone preferred to forget.

Innumerable images of Africa, photographs he had once viewed, and stories heard from others, passed through his mind; Gustavo Dores experienced the fullness of recollection. His emotions welled up. What effort! What enthusiasm! What dedication in the day-to-day work, in keeping the books in order! And he saw Castanheira persevering, Castanheira climbing the steps to the Ministry of Colonial Affairs every morning, in the person of the department head Gustavo Dores.

"Excuse me."

Gustavo Dores stepped aside to let the lady pass by. A blonde, heavy-set woman dressed in bright colors. Perfumed. He looked at her legs. Not bad. And there he was with the bouquet of flowers in his hand.

It was already late. Almost ten-thirty. No one was coming. That was obvious. And suddenly he had a great desire to leave. No. He would not go yet. He would wait a moment longer. He had come, he had fulfilled his duty. Again he felt a desire to draw back, to move to the edge of the tomb. He thought of Dona Conceição, and then, immediately, of Dona Conceição, heavy, quiet, faded, without any perfume, Dona Conceição as he had never seen her.

He grew frightened, he actually felt a strange fear. Although he had followed many women with his eyes, and at times with more than his eyes, such an ignominious image of Dona Conceição had never crossed his mind—on the contrary, he had always thought of her in the favorable light of thirty invisible and impalpable years of tranquillity. And now, suddenly, the years passed by all at once and nothing remained, everything disappeared, leaving the vacuum of a life that had slipped quietly by; in vain he searched for a pleasant memory that, in such a moment of anguish, would save him from his despair. Damned Castanheira! To hell with the old guy! He saw the sardonic laugh on his face, the unkempt beard, the dirty fingernails; he even heard the doltish snickering with which he had accompanied his own jokes. The life of a mountebank, going from place to place, his possessions on his back. Setting up his wares in order to rob the blacks. Fortunately, the law had been enforced which had brought all the riffraff under control. And "they," all the Castanheiras, led the troops to where they knew there would be elephant tusks—an avalanche of gigantic tusks roared through his mind—and, in the Metropolis, it was thought that authority had been flouted, as if such people, at that time, would go with flag held high to exchange cattle for glass beads! Those soldiers, yes, they went convinced, and they fought against hundreds of blacks. They didn't know the language of the heathens nor did the blackies know Portuguese— or everything would have been explained, and the Castanheiras, then. . . . He looked at the flowers. He was being unjust.

Seriousness existed, heroism existed. People are not to be judged by appearances, nor by what one hears, but by what they do. Those who hadn't come—true hypocrites. Nobody had come; if only someone would show up! But life is like that: a man works, makes sacrifices, and is forgotten. How many must have owed him money! They were afraid that, ten years later, Castanheira would still demand it back; he, who lived so unpretentiously but always paid for his own coffee! Unpretentiousness or stinginess? Economy isn't stinginess in a man who lives alone and has no family. Without anyone. . . . And, recovered now, relishing having his clothes in order, the mahogany bed, the wardrobe that had belonged to Aunt Edwiges (with a w), Dona Conceição's solicitude, the afternoons on the veranda, he felt immense compassion for Castanheira whose friendly grave nobody cared for, not even out of a forced sense of family responsibility, just because "it looks bad." But time was passing, he couldn't stay there forever. He smiled. He had time to stay there forever. And he went walking toward the cemetery's main road. He began to go up. He hadn't left the flowers. He would go back, put them on the grave, and depart. He stopped. Just then, he raised his eyes to the very end of the pavement. . . . and standing still at the summit, not knowing which way to turn, was Pereira Cláudio!

He threw himself into the space between two tombs. With some difficulty, because they were very close, he succeeded in squeezing in. Gasping for breath, covered with dust, stumbling and sinking in the raised earth—it was always muddy there, sticky mud!—he ran close to the tombs.

When he arrived at the edge of the last one, he peered out, trembling. Pereira Cláudio was in front of him. He couldn't leave the spot. The rabble! They stick their noses in everything! It figured: Cláudio, always a busybody, had not been shamed by the coolness of his words. As if he had some right to attend that very intimate homage, for friends only; a man who was in the Ministry strictly by fraud and who understood the overseas territories even less than the doorman. "Was it in Mozambique?" Namucala in Mozambique! What a dolt! And once stuck, unable to move a foot—gutless. He saw himself everywhere: a department head with ridiculous anxieties, committing blunders. Furious, capable of biting him, he again peered out. Pereira Cláudio, hesitant, had begun to go down another road. Idiot! Dores crossed the path in one leap and raced for the gate which he saw at the back. He passed many people, funeral processions were arriving; he slowed his pace. They were looking at him, he could guess what they must have been thinking about his frightened, dirty appearance; he brushed himself off a little. It seemed to him that everybody must be aware of the fiasco of the commemoration, of his flight. Ashamed, he wanted to walk quickly, which was worse, much more noticeable. He walked with his eyes down, afraid of meeting anyone he knew, anyone with whom he would be obliged to exchange a few words. As he approached the gate, when he was breathing a sigh of relief, there appeared at his side the fellow dressed in black, who was also leaving. The man looked at him with the look of a policeman and then, surprised, stared at the flowers. Gustavo Dores stopped. He had come away carrying the flowers. Suddenly he wished to be rid of everything, not to be there, nor in the department, nor at home, nor anywhere at all. He longed to disappear or to have the entire world disappear—"Do you want them?"—and he placed the flowers in the other man's hands.

A streetcar started up; and Gustavo Dores, instantaneously eager to run toward something, dashed to catch it. From the platform, he could still see the fellow turn around and disappear with the damned flowers into the crowd of people that was milling about the gate.

### III

Upon returning home at the end of the afternoon, shortly after leaving the office, he had made a firm decision not to go back to the café. Those men didn't deserve his company, poor devils without shame or initiative, incapable of understanding the very life they had lived. He had hesitated to appear at the Department so as not to meet Pereira Cláudio; but he hadn't seen him, obviously he hadn't seen him. He laughed several times at the trick he had played on him, hiding and afterwards openly departing behind his very back!

They hadn't run into each other. He had almost been looking forward to their paths crossing in the corridor, which was always an occasion for formal greetings. But he didn't seek him out; besides, he'd had no need to. The day had passed by without any news at all. Only Passos Silva solicitously asked about the commemoration. He had felt a jolt, but had recovered right away: "Very simple. Very simple." And the reply: "Allow me, Mr. Dores, not to believe your words." He had become exasperated: "You doubt me?" And Passos Silva had run to sit down at his desk, hurriedly dipping his pen while his colleagues smiled ironically. At that moment he had come to doubt that there was, among the whole lot of them, any understanding whatsoever. He was tempted to leave; but, thanks to the papers on his desk awaiting their proper handling, he was able to berate, with proper acrimony, one of his subordinates. And he knew them well enough to see that, on this occasion as on others, he had subjugated them totally.

He went up the steps, knocked on the door (he had the key, he was always concerned about taking it with him; nevertheless, during the day he always knocked). He had forgotten the butter! And Dona Conceição could not resist commenting: "You came home early, but you didn't remember to bring it."

"I told you I'd forget."

"Did you go to the cemetery?"

"What a question! Of course I went!"

"Was it pretty?"

"Pretty!? Is there anything beautiful about such things?"

## *IV*

It was when he sat down at the table and noticed the empty vases that he remembered the flowers. A difficult moment made worse by the timely arrival of his daughter who was coming from her "rehearsal": "Go on, Papa, tell me how it went? Did you give a speech, Papa?"

There had been no speeches. And that's just as well because nobody listens to them. "Oh, Mimi, speeches for whom?"— and he smiled to himself, privately, pleased with his clever response. Nevertheless, an uneasiness persisted: it had become impossible to get rid of the image of the strange fellow, one moment crossing his path and the next with his face bent over the flowers.

After dinner he sat on the veranda, taking in the fresh air. Carefully he rolled a cigarette and lit it. He didn't smoke except after dinner; the tobacco was even in the pocket (the right-hand pocket) of the jacket he wore around the house. Inside, his daughter had turned on the radio. Dona Conceição never got involved with the apparatus; she confined herself to listening, commenting on this or that phrase, this or that song. One day she had requested that they play some songs from her time. They were not on records. She had already forgotten her musical nostalgia when she had been pleasantly surprised by a live program in which some old waltzes had been performed ("Performed, Mother," Mimi had emphasized) on the piano. Since then she felt a great respect for the apparatus and ceased to consider it a stranger.

A few unconnected words from the radio reached Gustavo Dores. But who could that fellow have been? What matters is that you meet these people only once in your life!

"Father, come listen, come listen!"

". . . a simple homage in memory of an illustrious Africanist, Pereira Castanheira, who was one of the heroes of the

Campaigns of Occupation, defending Namucala against thousands of rebellious natives. Some of his friends gathered around his grave, among them our esteemed associate Mr. Gustavo Dores, a high-ranking government official, to whom we owe the brilliant idea for this touching ceremony. In his brief but moving extemporaneous remarks, Mr. Gustavo Dores traced the profile of the honored man, after which all those present marched in devout silence around the humble grave which they left strewn with flowers."

Dona Conceição looked at him, deeply touched. His daughter came over to give him a kiss. And Gustavo Dores, after worrying for one more instant about the whole event, thought: "Who knows whether the fellow knew Castanheira and went to lay the flowers there for him? Of course he didn't know him. He went to lay them at some other grave. Perhaps his wife's. Perhaps a beloved son's."

He felt happy. He wished he were in the café to confront Pinheiro Couto, the cynic of the group, with those words flowing through his mind: ". . . in his brief but moving extemporaneous remarks, Mr. Gustavo Dores traced the profile of the honored man, after which . . ."

1946                          *Translated by Edward V. Coughlin*

# The Russian Campaign

To die of old age is a rare, singular,
and extraordinary death, and far less
natural than the others; it is the last
and most extreme kind of dying.

*Montaigne, "On Age"*

W HEN I went to live on Cedofeita Street, in that house
with its small glazed door, deep corridor, immense staircase
with a very high banister, and bedrooms lining the corridor of
the second floor, I knew, of course, that the "spirits" of Oporto
were being officially invoked on a nearby street in which the
offices and meeting rooms of the Spiritist Society had been
installed, but I did not know that the same thing was taking
place on the ground floor of that house and that its tenants were
assiduous and homegrown practitioners of similar experiments.
I was living, at that time, in a state of penury, eating when I had
the money, owing rent on the room, studying in various cafés on
borrowed coffees, and desperately exploring along the streets a
solitude from which my friends, more comfortably ensconced in
life or in the pocketbooks of parents they still had and I no
longer did, could extract me. In fact, I was never popular with
my friends and had always received from strangers, or from
recent and casual friends, more intimate and delicate confidences
than those they had bestowed on me. If my friends respected and

still respect me, it is not from an intimacy that always constrained me and which I myself am incapable of reciprocating,
but from a loyalty and frankness, or, rather, from a simplicity
that, knowledgeable and experienced in all that life has to offer
of the terrible and sordid, is no less a constant surprise, however
wounded and pained, than the bitterness it is made of. But back
to the "spirits."

I used to buy cigarettes from a woman across the street
whose tobacco stand was set up in a doorway, as was the custom
in Oporto in those days. She was a tall and strong old woman,
always dressed in black, who wore on her head a black kerchief
the ends of which were tied at her chin. Her melancholy and
mournful air was, at the same time, unctuous and pallid, like
the polished surface that many elbows had produced on her
narrow little counter. Once, when I went to buy some "Defi-
nitivos," a feeble brand that marked my worse moments, she
was conversing with another old woman who sold greens further
on, in whose doorway stood crates with yellowed cabbages and
equally yellowed green beans. The other woman did not dress in
black, but in ample and colorful blouses and a filthy apron atop a
very fat ring of buttocks and skirts. They were complaining that
business was bad, they couldn't sell anything, nobody was sell-
ing anything. By the looks of it, people in that neighborhood
did not smoke, did not eat greens. This was what, butting into
their conversation, I told them.

The old woman in black raised her hands and her glance
and rolled her eyes upward. The fat woman looked me up and
down, outfitted in that rumpled and skimpy suit that had once
belonged to someone else but was then mine, and exchanged a
glance with the woman in black, who nodded her head and
confirmed: "Yes, he's one of those gentlemen who've moved in
across the street."

"Then you don't know, sir? You're a student, aren't you?"

"What don't I know?"

"Then you don't know that ever since the spirits moved here, nobody sells a thing anymore."

"What spirits?"

"Well! Right here, just around that corner, they've even set up a house for such things. And in the house where you live, sir, nobody lasts. You'll see. Those people downstairs spend their life at this. How do you expect anything to be sold? The atmosphere is so stormy that all business grinds to a halt."

The old woman in black agreed. Before, she used to sell a lot, the street was full of regular customers. Then the spirits came, and some tobacco shops were also opened on the street, nobody bought from her anymore. And it wasn't a matter, that much was clear, of competition. No it wasn't. Cigarettes are always the same, and people get used to buying them at the same spot. It was the spirits. Everybody was complaining. Business, a business you could make a living on, only past that block, down the street, far from the intersection.

I, who had spent years recovering from the fears with which, as a child, my family had planned the systematic and hygienic elimination of my terror of the dark and of inexplicable noises, I was appalled. Not at the economic correlation that might exist between small trade and the turbulence produced by the spirits the mediums invoked, but at the information that this was happening right under my feet, perhaps under my very room in whose wooden floor, full of holes, rarely did a night pass without my housemates managing to grind a foot of the bed into one of the holes, an act, incidentally, that we would all repeat, in a permanent vengeance devoid of imagination.

Devoid of imagination. I would see. And I did. Nights in that house began to be infernal. Howls, groans, doors slamming, even the classic dragging of chains along the corridor—in short, the trivia of horror stories, it all went on there. If they, out of a need for consolation, believed as I, out of fear, did not, it would all have lived up to the standard of my downstairs neighbors' wildest experimental longings. But in my case, being my own master, by temperament a loner, though very sociable on an occasional whim, and on top of all that afraid of the spirits in which I did not believe, it was obvious that my housemates could not avoid the voluptuous and tyrannical pleasure of instilling fear, which is a human consolation, independently of the respect and the esteem that, for other reasons, they might have for me—or even because of these. What had made me recount, with irony and some unease, the old women's conversation!

The solution would be to move out of the house. But I, in debt there, in debt at the house from which I had moved, a house that belonged to a sister of the woman who owned this one, and having no money with which to begin somewhere else, I could not, in fact, leave. Possibly the desire to cast out my discomforting penury played a part, unconsciously, in the plans of some of my housemates. Everything is possible, without our even needing to suspect that malice might enter into it.

I turned into more of a vagrant. To roam the streets at night, kilometer upon kilometer, began to be, more than it already had been, my life. I barely slept by day. And then, the nights were, after all, more useful to me for writing. Reading, writing, anxiously following on the newspaper hoardings the campaigns in Russia, sleeping on benches in public parks (very thin, in a green coat, eyes sparkling, and a head of hair white as snow, the old man approached me like an arrow, sat down, and asked me sprightly: "You tired? You sleepy? You shouldn't sleep on a park bench. The humidity isn't good for you! Wouldn't you like to come have a drink?" And I got up and fled without looking back), listening to the sewers flowing beneath the sidewalks (on the parapet, lights from the opposite bank were shining in a whitish halo, and from a shadow leaning against the parapet a voice called out to me: "Pst. . . Pst. . . You, sir . . ." and I lowered my eyes and saw an enormous leg, purple, with a wound that had concentric circles of scaly and suppurating skin, and I gave him a coin jealously deducted from my next day's bread), moving among the tall buildings, among the tides of ancient windows that peered over the pavement, with gloomy doors that opened from upstairs at the pull of a cord (in the room we took, the partition was made of thin wood and you could hear the wheezing of the springs and metal in the bed next door, and as I dug my nails into her shoulders I felt that the crawling sensation along my legs was bedbugs), wandering by the riverbank (I saw a man's switchblade gleam and heard the dull thud of the body in the alley, and the sailor came running by me, blade in hand, and grabbed my arm and threw me against the wall, snarling at me: "You didn't see a thing"—and the women let out a hideous wail), contemplating in fascination the wide mouth of the tunnel being carved into the hillside (and after trying, for nights, to harangue them with politics, two of them held me while a third took my watch, and they ran off), going down steps and more steps (in the shadow of the bridge, the canvas chair was set up in the street, and the boy, ashen-faced, coughed and spat, for inside the house there was neither light nor air enough for him to die), losing myself in the crowd (the plaza was a sea of people carrying lighted candles, and all were singing: "Ave, Ave"), eating some small sandwiches at the tavern where you always tripped on the very high and worn-out step (the boy, when I was leaving, would stare at me and hold out his hand . . .).

During the Carnival holidays the house emptied, the "spirits" quieted down. But I could no longer tolerate any world. And, on Tuesday, at night, I didn't eat even the sandwich, but went to a movie. In the lobby they were dancing. In the poorly lit room, during the tiresome and almost constant intermissions, they threw streamers and little paper bags, and a lady bombarded me from the loge. She had an enormous but attractive bosom, which threatened to escape her dress. Each time she threw a streamer at me, with the other hand she held in her charms. I ostentatiously walked along the corridor. She did not emerge from her box, the door of which was open. I left, and walked across the city toward my house. Along Cedofeita Street, pools of water gathered in the irregular flagstones of the sidewalk. I put the key in the door, felt the usual shudder as I entered, and, as I start up the first flight of stairs, I hear a racket at the next door neighbors', their door opens and the woman comes directly to me, bathed in tears, shouting: "Ai, my precious daddy!"—and right behind her, her husband, shouting: "Ludovina! Ludovina! Don't talk to him or you'll spoil it all!"

I don't know how, but I was already halfway in the street, and then the sycamores, the prison, the street that curved at its end, the parapet, the lights of the opposite bank, pst, pst, the stairs, the Infante Don Henrique was born there, the wharf, the wharf, the ramp, the plaza (the children were carrying the other child to the cemetery in a casket, and I saw them again as they crossed in front of me, all in white), at the door of the São João Theater a group of boys was having trouble squeezing a woman's bottom into a luxury car, water from the fire hydrants ran down Santo António Street, the Clerigos' Tower was silhouetted in the distance (I had given five milreis to the guard and had taken her to visit the Tower and was seated with her in my lap when I heard footsteps on the staircase, and it was her husband, who asked me to continue), and the sycamores once again. I sat down on a bench. From the bandstand there came a hushed clamor. I approached. The small door to the cellar was ajar, a sliver of light emerged with the voices. I peered in. In the middle of a circle of boys, the old man with the green coat was dancing, naked in his green coat. He saw me and recognized me. I don't know what he said. A roar of laughter broke out and at once caused the light of the lamp and the inflamed faces that surrounded him to flicker. I crossed the park. I ran. In the depths of the café the same lamp shone, hanging from the wall. I walked among the stacks of tables. Only one of the tables was in service, in the back close to the counter, and from it two long-forgotten and emaciated old men, with thin greasy hair, stared at me. One of them was leaning against the wall, an arm on the table and the other across the back of the chair. The second man, seated sideways, was staring at me while the first resumed the vague expression he had had as he conversed. At the counter, the waiter, resentfully, heated some coffee for me. The old man leaning against the wall kept quiet in the face of the second man's insistent repetition: "On those plains, and what plains they are . . . you see, my friend?"

And, as I drank my coffee, the first man said softly: "What about the snow? What about the snow? Just think of the snow! So much equipment lost, buried in the snow . . ." and the second nodded his head in agreement, beneath the eye of the waiter who was picking up my coins.

I left. The sole sign of morning was the streetlamps being turned off, in sections, as I proceeded, leaving behind me a darkness from which I tried to flee, running to keep up with the rhythm of the electrician who, far away, I don't know where, was moving from one switch to another.

1946–1960                    *Translated by Daphne Patai*

# Kama and the Genie

> He is never seen, but is the Seer; He
> is never heard, but is the Hearer; He is
> never thought of, but is the Thinker;
> He is never known, but is the
> Knower. There is no other seer than
> He, there is no other hearer than He,
> there is no other thinker than
> He, there is no other knower than
> He. He is your Self.
>
> Brihadaranyaka Upanishad

HE was a very old genie, as old as genies can be. And he
had always lived in that gigantic banyan tree at the entrance to
the village. An immensely vast and thick tree, with numerous
ample, tall, and spreading branches, where he had been able to
settle down and raise an enormous family. From that spot,
through the years, he had seen the little village grow and age
and remain its very same self beside the river. Or, rather, at the
beginning of his life he had encountered the fortunate combination of such a comfortable tree and of a group of houses which,
though very sparse then, showed that the inhabitants were not
so poor as not to feed him with relative decency; and there he
stayed. Afterwards, in fact, the village had not grown as much
as it had promised at that time; but he had grown inseparably
fond of the tree and even—why not say so?—of those people, a

bit withdrawn and overly stingy, who nonetheless believed in him and his powers. From his observation posts in the recesses of the monstrous trunk or among the powerful roots that rose like shadowy walls, or even in the highest branches where he held sway over the whole village and the countryside up to the bend in the river, he amused himself with the life of his subjects.

When settling in, he had been obliged to prove his tutelary presence with some well-worn ruses (although old ones and known to them). Later, those ostentatious demonstrations became unnecessary; and from time to time, just for security and prestige—so they would not suppose he had deserted the tree— with the passing of the seasons and years he confided to his descendants the responsibility of shaking the branches when no wind blew, of whispering secrets into the ears of passing villagers, or even, but this very rarely, of suddenly stopping, as if frozen in air, someone who passed by distractedly, without paying his respects, or some forgetful villager who was behind in his obligatory offering of milk, sugar, sesame, and honey. This combination, left in small bowls among the roots of the tree, was his official repast, and it was his duty to demand it, despite the agony that such a mixture caused him. What he really liked was a small chicken wing, rice with butter, and the distilled liquor of a virgin palm. But these things were quite rare among the villagers' gifts, except during the Festival of Lights. For these and other reasons most of his descendants had abandoned him, left the tree, departed in search of better villages. And, wandering during the afternoons along the veins dry of sap, or staring from the top at the tree's dim core, he pondered that only the dullest of the children and grandchildren remained, creatures useful solely for tasks of daily subsistence. This he would never say, not even in his old-timer's mutterings; but he thought it. And this thinking, which his descendants, even if they were slow-witted, could read in him with the particular omniscience of the species, did nothing to calm his inner life: it was enough to see how they slipped away from his presence, confining themselves to the more distant regions, always in secret conspiracies totally lacking in danger—for he too knew everything. But more than once, catching him distracted, they had tried to provoke him with villagers practicing unexpected absurdities. And it was certainly from these family rebellions that came his reputation as an eccentric, which he didn't deserve, but that he heard the villagers allude to when, with a touch of pride, they showed the gigantic tree to a stranger who would soon hurry back bearing a substantial offering of the sickening food.

But the most interesting spectacle of his long life, absorbing his attentions unceasingly and entertainingly, lay "beneath" (in relation to his genie's world) the short life of the mortals he observed. Through the decades and centuries, always in permanent contact with the village, a village very isolated from others, he ended up knowing all the souls contained in that small parcel of humanity. And among these, in spite of the simple life that was lived there, very few were those who had disappeared by ascending to the Supreme Good. The great majority, held to the earth by their sins, deficiencies, and distractions in the daily ritual, remained in the village after death overcame them, and their bodies were consumed by the fire of which, from his tree, he could see only the smoke that rose whitened from the sides of the cemetery toward the blue sky. (He knew the cemetery perfectly from the descriptions of it provided him by its resident demons, who at times came to the tree to visit, for a chat among unoccupied folk in such a small village.) Of course, the souls didn't know one another directly, or even themselves. He, however, knew them all, beneath the wrappings of flesh in which they took shelter to continue the earthly existence to which they had come. What was entertaining was precisely the wrapper.

For the wrappers were totally unpredictable, befitting Nature's current supply and according to the load of sins and deficiencies to be expiated. And the resulting accidents were always unforeseen. When the thin trail of smoke rose in the air, he, who had already noted who had died and knew his least habits, began to wait. . . . And not long thereafter, from some lair, life would begin for a rat, ant, lizard, the gods know what, which he immediately recognized. A terribly miserly and suspicious old man, who many times had threatened to cut down his tree (the thought itself made him shiver), reappeared changed into a dog. But instead of being a tame and respectful dog, it was always raising its leg against the tree. It later died, run over by a cart, and then reappeared as a rat. This rat worried him with its insistence on wanting to settle into the tree, in the deep hollows among the roots. He had to mobilize his whole family to demand respect from it. Of course, one day, after being tortured to death by the group of boys who hunted it (and who had hidden behind the tree to do so prohibited a thing), it came back as a lizard, repugnant and crippled. This time it seemed to have learned its lesson. And he even permitted the animal, despised by all its equals and suffering with love for a female lizard who lived near the tree, to climb clumsily up the branches from where it could contemplate—breathless and tearful—its beloved, who didn't even want to know that it was looking at her. And thus it died, from hunger and bad luck, for it was very weak and on one occasion fell to the ground and there remained, to die. It now became an immensely wise cat, which wouldn't even hunt a small mynah that landed at its foot, and lived in continuous meditation, lying virtuously at the door of the house belonging to one of its grandsons (grandson of the old man the genie had met when he moved into the tree). It could be expected to regain human form.

Very entertaining it was, too, using his genie's omniscience and memory, to identify these transmigrations of souls with the human and animal genealogies of that small world. And also the vicissitudes that the incarnations passed through. The oxcart driver's cat who was the dog's son turned up at his uncle's house as a parrot, who was the father of the ox who was the son of the washerwoman who was born from the cat, grandfather of the first cat, and from a serpent who was herself the ox's aunt. Only he knew these spiritual relationships and only he, with his immediate consciousness of the invisible to which they pertained, could trace them. None of the souls knew this at all, except through rare and fleeting intuitions which they, captive to flesh, could not interpret, or purely as theory which they indeed interpreted as best they could while they were human. Often, he heard near him the villagers (whom he knew as their own ancestors or as animals that gathered around them), certain that the tree's shadow inspired them, making the most comical conjectures about their past or future lives. Or, better said, only about their past lives, because despite their display of humility they always imagined that they would gain access to heaven.

In all this the genie did not interfere in any way. He was— and well he knew it—a simple tree genie, without even the vast powers that those bumpkins imagined him to have. And for this very reason (though it was difficult for him to admit the truth) he was possibly guilty of the irritable character attributed to him, given that, as has been said, the most disagreeable and above all outrageous tricks played on the villagers were not his. Not that at one time or another he might not have played them. But he had always bitterly repented, for he was a peaceful genie who fulfilled his obligations (of which there were none beyond his mere existence) and greatly respected the hierarchy. And he had repented because those tricks, always unjustly irritating to those affected, had contributed to their regression within the chain of beings. And that his influence could be negative in the most disappointing ways, and provoke the gods' anger, he had learned in a frightful manner. He still trembled, and his genie's conscience grew clouded—imagine!—just to recall the incident.

Once, late at night, he had been awakened by a sweet murmur next to his tree. His sensibilities soon recognized who was speaking. It was the shoemaker's youngest son, a terrible boy who, though very young, had ruined the majority of the village virgins. And the daughter of a woodsman who lived in the forest and whose family rarely came to the village. He knew by heart what they were saying. And also what the boy wanted, though, exposed as the genie was at the entrance to the village, this was something he had only rarely actually been able to observe. She refused, shaking, defending herself from the youth's embraces; but it was obvious that her resistance was weakening, her aroused flesh was betraying her, was abandoning her, tearfully, to the arms of the scoundrel. What to do? The temptation to watch it all was great. For love, even the most vile, rules the world and is one of the most beautiful things in the universe, so it is said. But virtue and the sacrament of marriage and virginity are essential to the social order. Now, a tree genie belongs, ultimately, much more to the social order than to the erotic order of the World. And so he interfered. The tree gave a terrifying crack. One of the highest and largest branches broke off and, falling accurately, hit the youth without touching the damsel. And all his genie's prescience couldn't prevent what happened next. She, who was at first paralyzed, watching the branch and then the bloody body that fell at her feet, let out a cry and moaning with desperation threw herself on the corpse—for it was now a corpse—shaking it, embracing it, and rubbing against it as if wanting the dead youth to possess her with the same ardor with which, when alive, he had held her in his arms. The genie looked on, horrified, not knowing what to do. And there was no time. For a tiger jumped out of the shadows, an enormous tiger, and on the spot tore the girl to pieces. The tree shook with a fearful roar that made the genie and his frightened family retreat into its deepest roots. And there in a lightning bolt, blinding even for genies, stood the god Kama, blazing with fury before him, upbraiding him in the most inconceivable curses and the most unimaginable obscenities.

The tree had taken a long time to recover from the bolt that had hit it. For a long time, too, he hadn't even dared emerge from the roots through the sap canals that tasted charred. Generations had passed, certainly, during his afflicted seclusion. And that was what distracted him and brought him back to his daily inactivity, making him delay longer, day by day, in his observation posts. For it was as if the descent of the god Kama had greatly confused the transmigration of souls. Or else he, who in his humble genie's life had never seen a god, had become a little confused. Which was only natural, as he was told by one of the cemetery demons with whom he had grown more friendly and who traveled a lot (or so he said, for the omniscience of tree genies can't penetrate the malice of such beings).

The distraction of returning to his routine (and the village's routine had also been disturbed, with interminable penances, by the bolt that had struck the tree) had been of short duration, especially at night. Because his victim's soul had not been reincarnated. After a long period in limbo, it had begun circling the tree, moaning as if scratching at the trunk with its spirit's fingernails. He hadn't seen the young girl's soul again; but the demon told him that she was a pullet in her father's coop. And the tiger, who could it be? It wasn't a soul he knew, so he supposed, though he had not had time to look at it carefully. The demon didn't know either. But they both agreed that it must certainly be some ancestor of the young girl who, in a moment of inner illumination, had come to prevent her from the horrible crime of sinning with a corpse.

As far as the villagers were concerned, there had been merely the bolt that had wounded the tree and killed the two young people. The bolt had come, according to them, because

the two sweethearts had defiled the sacred tree with their rap-
tures; and also because that stain had been greatly augmented by
the extremely condemnable fact that the two were from different
castes. He, who had seen Brahmins' souls become dogs', then go
from dogs to Kshatriyas, to Vaishyas and to casteless persons
and, at times, become Brahmins again by mere chance of circumstances, smiled at this excessively ingenuous hypothesis,
for he knew quite well the reason (and then he trembled) that he
had nearly been fulminated, or as much as a genie can be, by the
bolt. But it all ended with offerings of that sickening hodgepodge in such quantities that, afterwards, it was the sour smell
of it that still tormented him the most.

If it had not been for a loafing snake who during this time
had settled in among the roots of the tree and done him the favor
of eating it all up, the environs, smelly from the excess of food
rotting in the sun, would have been intolerable. And the serpent
had freed him from that stubborn, suffering soul which was like
an unpleasant memory of his inopportune deed. It freed him in a
way that was very simple, but nonetheless beyond the reach of
his powers as a tree genie. Just how the curious phenomenon
had occurred, however, his omniscience could not recall. Much
as he might concentrate, he could not remember. His demon
friend, who had also made great efforts, but to no avail, to
convince the suffering soul to wander in the cemetery (where,
after all, the ashes rested of the person it had last been), had held
the opinion that the whole episode, including the serpent, was
still the work of the god Kama.

And precisely at a moment when they were discussing this
matter the serpent and the soul had disappeared. They had
both—he and the demon—been stupefied at the event and the
very simple way it happened. But the demon too did not remember (or pretended not to remember, because the malice of
these beings is great, even toward friendly genies).

An intense commotion woke him from these meditations. A group of men was dragging another man who was struggling violently. He immediately recognized him (or, rather, recognized the youth's soul) in a tremor that shook the tree leaves. For it had finally become, now, a dreadful thief whom the people had been hunting. It wasn't for that, however, that he trembled. But from the inevitable that was going to happen: they would come to cut down one of his straightest and strongest trunks to impale the thief, according to law and custom. A new tremor, all irony, shook the banyan. That's when he suddenly imagined the look on the god Kama's face on hearing the proclamation that condemned the thief to be impaled, in the name of the King.

An imperceptible crack of the trunk and the darkening of the horizon still brought to his mind his lowly station as village tree genie. And it was head down and humble that he replied to his demon friend's "good afternoon," as he hurried, rubbing his hands together, to tell him that there was going to be a capital execution in the cemetery. The genie was very old, unrespected and abandoned by his descendants, old and wanting only to have nothing to do, either from near or far, with the gods that had taken control of the world, relegating genies like himself and demons like his friend to the last rung, reduced to inactivity or to the most sordid duties. Respectively, it must be said.

The demon, however, was enthusiastic. Now it was assured and guaranteed that that soul would haunt the cemetery restlessly, bringing a new change to the disconsolate environment in which nothing ever happened. Insistently, he invited the genie to come along, to attend this rare spectacle. Rare indeed. That both could remember, in their lifetimes it had happened only once or twice, because the village was small, isolated, and, being poor, did not attract thieves or criminals. And as for crimes and thefts punishable by death, there was no one in the village who would commit them. For this very

reason the village was strangely agitated, swept through by a
fervor of justice. So great that it had repercussions even inside
the tree, which was calmness itself. He hesitated. Would he go?
Wouldn't he go? To go out in the open air and risk catching
some chill, or that his descendants might occupy the place in his
absence, or that the tree, old as it was, might fall down rotten if
he abandoned it—all this, and his old habits too, held him
there. But the execution was a rare spectacle, and this one had a
very special relish. The demon suggested to him that for the trip
to the cemetery, and even for watching the execution from a
privileged position, he had a recourse like no one else: he had
only to take advantage of the wood they were going to cut from
him. It was, in fact, a way of traveling safely to the cemetery and
an opportunity that had never before arisen for him to attend the
torture *de visu,* feeling and seeing the man descend, with cries,
upon the genie's own length, while his soul struggled, knowing
the punishment that awaited it. But this, in his goodness,
horrified him. And how would he return? Yes, how would he
return? On foot, the demon told him, soon adding that he
would accompany him to help him return more quickly once the
execution was over. He still hesitated. And thus matters stood
when he saw the woodsmen draw near, pay their respects, and
the oldest of them advance further and address him, asking
pardon for the inconvenience they would cause him by cutting
down a small trunk. And with blows that reverberated painfully
in his rheumatic joints, they began to cut off the trunk from
which on the spot they would carve the stake for the execution.
When the trunk was nearly cut, the genie leaped forward and
embarked on it.

In his excitement, the paring of the trunk to give it the
prescribed shape and diameter, and their sharpening of it, was
almost fun, also because the demon kept telling him that justice
required great dispatch in the man's execution, before an order
of general amnesty could arrive marking the coronation of the

crown prince, since it was known that the old king had died. And if they didn't kill that dangerous thief in time, they would have to let him go free. The carrying of the trunk to the place of execution, in the slow steps of the ritual, was very pleasant. But the cemetery, at whose entrance they were going to position it, seemed to the genie a sad place, abandoned and dirty. Still, he would not stay there long. The men set the stake and went away. And he remained there, a bit squeezed on the erect and pointed pale. But, contrary to his fears, the night hours provided a continuous distraction. The demons, pleased by his unheard-of presence, sang, danced, told stories, and organized a banquet in which he enjoyed his wine and a small chicken wing. Cock or hen? And a shudder ran through him as he remembered that the young girl, in that other time, was a pullet. Feeling somewhat indisposed, he called aside his friend the demon and confided his doubts to him. Which cock or hen had that well-roasted wing that he had eaten come from? All the others heard his question and understood his worry. Laughter raced through the circle of demons. There was no danger at all: even if she were still gallinaceous, and even if the wing had been hers (and it wasn't), do souls stay in roasted wings? And they roared like the condemned that they were. He also laughed. And laughed again when one of the demons told how the village had placed a group of men on the road to the forest, charged with meeting and distracting the city messenger, should he meanwhile arrive. With this delay, the thief would certainly be executed and upon being pardoned after death, would receive a decent burial, much to his soul's advantage. This the villagers thought; but some of the demons thought differently. For the villagers, although like everyone else very knowledgeable about ritualistic intricacies, were wrong on one point. And this point would guarantee the possession of that soul by the demons under any circumstances. As a matter of fact, the executed man who enjoys posthumous amnesty does have his soul rise high on the scale of perdition; and even higher if there is time to fulfill the ritual accurately with funeral honors for the corpse. But with this one the case was not so simple. And the demons' redoubled laughter, echoing in the distracted and pleasurable giddiness of palm liquor that he had abused, was like a juridical enlightenment: the delay that the villagers planned would only be legal if the messenger brought the order verbally, in which case, as the personal bringer of the word, any delay would be his own responsibility. Since they were used to receiving only tax collectors, who acted verbally, the villagers had forgotten that an amnesty is a written order. Once written and sealed, if it is then delayed the responsibility does not fall to the messenger. Since they were themselves responsible, they could not deliberately carry out the sentence before making an express inquiry to the central government. And, prior to all this, it would be legally and ritually impossible to take the man off the stake where he would be impaled. In spite of his omniscience, the genie was amazed at the demons' subtlety. And it was then that the first early morning cold began to be felt.

The cortege was now approaching the stake, with a large mass of people accompanying it. In front, with the executioner and his assistant and the village chief, came the condemned man, wearing a short tunic, the only attire permitted for the execution, and with his hands tied behind his back. Then two more assistants came, carrying the necessary benches on their heads; and another two carting the two iron weights that would be attached to his feet. The village guru went ahead to sprinkle the stake and surroundings with holy water. And the demons who stayed near the stake, whispering in a happy agitation that raised small dusty whirlwinds, were obliged to draw back. The genie was alone, inside the stake, and with that crowd before him. The executioner and the village chief, in accord with the legal norms, raised the condemned man's tunic and both verified by eyes and hands that he had not put on a slat or any other object to impede the torture. Then, while the executioner and his assistant tied the weights to his feet, the other two assistants placed the two benches into position, one on each side of the post. Turning the condemned man toward the crowd and holding him forcefully because he was twisting and shouting (gagged, he couldn't speak), the four raised him in the air to set him on the pale. Aghast, the genie saw the dark thighs and the darker parts that fear contracted as they came closer to his point.

That was when the genie was shaken by vomiting, as if the chicken wing were fluttering within him. The shuddering was such that the executioners let the man go, and as he fell to the ground an awestruck clamor rose from the fleeing multitude. The man got up, but with his hands tied behind his back could not take off the rope that tied the weights to his feet. He twisted in anguish, sweat running down him, and it was such and so much that the smell reached the genie inside the wood, in spite of how accustomed he was to the smell of the villagers, very careless in their ritual ablutions. The genie could not resist; he jumped out of the wood and as quickly as he could helped the thief to free himself. And while still busy undoing a knot, he could already just make out the light-colored soles of feet leaping in the distance in flight. At that very instant he felt a terrifying blow, and then others: the demons, furious, were giving him a first-class thrashing. He fainted.

And when he came to, he was inside the tree. But it wasn't the same tree, nor did the same beings surround it caressingly. He himself, although still feeling sore, was not the same. Strong, virile, bubbling with sap, he abandoned himself to the embraces of the young dryads who surrounded him. When they were exhausted and left, he got up to peep around. He was on a temple patio. And judging by the indecent sculptures on the walls, it was a temple to Kama.

He sighed in relief, content with his promotion. But as he breathed in, a nausea ran through him. He didn't need to look to know that, next to the tree, there, like everywhere else after all, was the same inevitable hodgepodge.

At nightfall, when the patio emptied and shadows began to gather in the halls and among the high reliefs, he, perched on one of the leafy branches, saw a glow coming from the sanctuary. He fidgeted restlessly while his dryads trilled crystalline laughter. The brightness came close to the tree, beat on its trunk as if with knuckles and, before vanishing, said:

"You freed me from a tight spot. . . . For that I've pardoned you."

With the confidence that he suddenly felt, the genie cried:

"But must I always have the same thing to eat?"

The god, however—now a drunken-like figure submerged in his nightly adventures—did not reply.

But from the depths of the tree there arose a delicious perfume. It came from his dryads who, in procession, were bringing him a very golden and fragrant little chicken wing.

1964                                    *Translated by K. D. Jackson*

# A Night of Nativity

> If God descends in person to human-
> ity, he abandons the dwelling that is
> his. With that one step, the universe
> is shaken. Let us alter the universe in
> its slighted part, and the whole edi-
> fice crumbles.
>
> *Celsus, cited by Origen in*
> Contra Celsum

## I

*I*T was as if the night, in its blackness, were merely the rumblings of the unseen waves against the base of the escarpment and the cold breeze that was salty to the mouth and nostrils and biting to the ears and gaps among the curls of his forehead. Wrapped in a woolen mantle, he could feel nothing else; and his eyes, absorbed steadfastly in the wide expanse beyond the parapet, opaque and without horizon, sought out nothing, merely stretched along the distance the images that filled his vague memory.

"Marcus Sempronius. . . ."

He turned and only then heard, over the roar of the unseen waves, the panting footsteps that had preceded the cry. In the indistinct light which emerged diffusely between the columns of the palace, he recognized the beard of Quintilius Verus; images in his memory, ebbing also to his limbs, reminded him of the boat, of the swimming exercises through the grottoes, of the oars slapping against the transparent water, and of a slave's corpse, from which, in the depth of the blue, a red cloud dispersed.

"What is it?"

Quintilius Verus tried to read in the man's face a disposition to listen to him. But, regardless, there was in the restlessness that agitated his whole body the resolve to speak.

"The fishermen of Aqua Livia, you know, Marcus Sempronius, those of Aqua Livia" (and in his tedium Marcus Sempronius visualized the small beach with young boys leaping about among the leaping fish), "when they rounded the cape, tonight, they heard. . . ."

"They heard what?" and the voice trailed off in the distance, distractedly, crested by the darting clarity of the sand on the small beach.

"They heard a voice shouting, no, not shouting, but crying out, howling, it was a sad wailing, deep in the night, above the cape, or from within it. . . ."

Marcus Sempronius, as if to draw out the halting narrative, began to cross the flagstone terrace. Next to the statue of Eros, which rose at the base of the steps of the colonnade, he turned, one of his sandals on the first step.

Quintilius Verus, with his wavering walk, approached slowly. Marcus Sempronius, looking over him to the darkness of the night beyond the parapet, smiled, twisting his lips.

"Marcus Sempronius . . . they heard a voice that said . . ." and Quintilius Verus, forgetful of the social conventions, which brought a furtive raising of Marcus Sempronius's eyebrow, sat down, head bowed, on the first step, next to the sandal with the gold laces.

"They heard a voice, then. And what did the voice say?" asked Marcus Sempronius, looking at the nape of the fisherman's curved neck.

Quintilius Verus was twisting his hands. Marcus Sempronius began to feel a slight discomfort, like nausea, and suddenly sensed a chill licking at his depilated legs. He pulled the mantle closer about him and climbed the stairs.

The voice of the other man called to him as he brushed the marble column and caught his mantle on some thorns of the rosebush that encircled it.

"Marcus Sempronius. . . . Warn the emperor. . . . They heard it say . . . it was the cape that spoke . . . that he was dead. . . ."

Marcus Sempronius stopped without turning around.

"Marcus Sempronius, don't leave me with this news. Nor tell the emperor that I brought it. They heard it say that the Great God Pan has died."

Marcus Sempronius turned around, descended the stairs to the statue, rested his head on Eros's hips, and asked:

"The Great God Pan?"

Quintilius Verus did not answer.

"But the gods don't die, Quintilius Verus, the gods are immortal."

"I know, Marcus Sempronius; I know, for I'm devout. But that's what they heard. And the voice howled so much that it must be true."

Marcus Sempronius approached the crouching figure. Beneath his mantle, without loosening it, he took coins from his pocket that tinkled on the flagstone.

"Go, Quintilius Verus, and don't repeat that story to anyone. And tell the fishermen of Aqua Livia not to repeat it either or the emperor will have them put to death for blasphemy."

And Marcus Sempronius climbed the stairs and entered the palace.

## II

In the great hall, illuminated by flaming torches, Marcus Sempronius made his way slowly among the scattered cushions,

stepping carefully over the legs of an outstretched and naked
slave—who must have already been dead—and lay down,
spreading out his mantle, next to the emperor. His gaze wandered from the aged face of Caesar to another slave, also naked,
who hung in front of them suspended by his feet from an iron
rod, with the tips of his fingers lightly brushing the marble
pavement. Once more, Marcus Sempronius verified that the
body of a man, thus suspended and bloodless, had a strange
beauty it would not have under other circumstances, no matter
how beautiful it was. And this one was. The images that had
hovered in the night, beyond the parapet, took shape now in
memories of that once living body, vigorous, young, so sub-
missive and supple, and which he himself had surrendered to
the emperor. Concentrating his gaze, he examined him minutely, detaining his eyes on the small cut on his neck, from
which, trickling up his head—he smiled at the inversion of
terms that the suspended body imposed—the blood dripped
dark into a silver basin lying between his dangling hands. For an
instant only, he wondered why he had overlooked the basin, had
not seen it when he sat down, only the hands, nothing else.
Certainly the hands looked alive, and indeed were still alive. He
felt a pleasurable shiver, an anticipated and delightful longing
for those hands that were dying. He sighed.

The emperor slept, breathing easily, ridiculously disar-
rayed, and on the ground was his dagger, caked with blood.
Marcus Sempronius bent down, grasped the dagger, wiped it on
Tiberius's tunic, laid it once again on the ground and arose.
Giving the emperor a sidelong glance, he clapped his hands.
Two slaves appeared with a stone and a rope, which they tied to
the feet of the cadaver over which Marcus Sempronius had
stepped.

And, carrying him, they exited to the terrace. Marcus
Sempronius waited, erect, without looking at the emperor,
until they returned, then dismissed them with a gesture.

He sat down again, half reclining. And passed the time watching the emperor who, with semi-closed eyes that shone fleeting, now only pretended to sleep. How old he was, full of creases on his neck and body! How very much he looked like an emaciated and exhausted Silenus! How the wrinkles and folds of his jowls seemed, by their weight, further to stretch the skin of his cranium, which shone bright with sweat beneath his sparse hairs! How his nose looked like a trunk or his sex, and how his sex looked like a nose! Feigning solicitude and love, he loosened his cape and with it covered the emperor. Tiberius opened his eyes, smiled at him, adjusted his body beneath the cape. His thin and sagging lips, which appeared drained of their fleshiness, opened slightly.

"Thank you, Marcus Sempronius. What would become of me without your thoughtful care?"

Marcus Sempronius lowered his eyes modestly, and said: "You well know, Caesar, that life means nothing to me except in your service."

"And it's not easy to serve me, it's not easy," and his voice grew bitter as he added, "Even I am fed up with serving me!" And then, with a trace of humor, he continued: "But then, it's been almost seventy years I've had to put up with me, and you, Marcus Sempronius, have had only ten years."

"It's as if it were yesterday."

"And that's true, because I esteem you. But it's equally true because on this island and in this palace, you and I have erased time. Thanks to us, time does not pass. Or it passes as the waves do, always the same and always different, but in the same sea. We have no rivers on this island, Marcus Sempronius. And what are rivers but time passing by? When you ordered tossed into the sea just now the slave, whose death brought me some pleasure, so very little, I felt clearly how not even with death does time pass here. Or it doesn't pass precisely because it is death. Notice, Marcus Sempronius, that blood dripping. It's as though life were draining out in the water that drips from the clepsydra, and death were draining out, and with it time, in that blood trickling, drop by drop, from a human clepsydra turned upside down. When blood pulses through our veins, it is time passing by. When it trickles like that, it is the time that remains."

"But, Caesar, why do you not open your veins so that, with your blood, time will run out?"

The eyes of Tiberius looked at Marcus Sempronius ironically.

"Because, if I opened them or ordered them opened, I would be the same as that slave you gave me. I would be someone, a being, an animal, to whom I, as emperor, brought death. And the last thing I desire, Marcus Sempronius, and that is why I let the Empire govern itself, is to be emperor of myself."

"You have always governed the Empire, Caesar."

"Yes, in truth I always have. But the only way I can manage it is to govern from afar. I grew tired of betrayals, of treachery, of ambitions, of struggles, of imperial pomp, of the priests, the family, everything. In the middle of it all, I could neither govern nor be myself. Thus, on this island, which is like the end of the world, I am the emperor for them, the ideal emperor, the invisible emperor, who allows them to do all the evil they want and all the good they desire, in my name, and whose sacred pronouncements at times descend upon them like a divine voice. My decrees are like the shower of gold that impregnated Danae. And the legend of my cruelty and debauchery here, magnified by ignorance and by their own fantasies—which are as fecund as mine, but lacking the freedom I have to effect them—only serves to heighten my transformation into a fearful and distant god who lives in their imaginations. As for me, I've never felt more human."

He looked once more, with weary fascination now, at the basin where the blood was thickly coagulating.

"The poets say, Marcus Sempronius, that those whom the gods love die young. Do you believe that I loved that slave? He was beautiful, young, intelligent—did you know he was intelligent?—and there he is suspended, draining himself as submissively as a lamb that doesn't understand why it is being sacrificed by the haruspex. For it's true, I loved him very much; and I'd like to believe that he was one of the few people, admitting that a slave is a person, who at times forgot I was the emperor. Probably the gods loved him, because I've never believed that men, and I'm a man, could become gods."

"Then you were the instrument of the gods' love, Caesar Augustus."

"I was, Marcus Sempronius, and not in vain."

Marcus Sempronius leaned back, his eyes closed. Tiberius sat up, and looked upon him. Without opening his eyes, Marcus Sempronius asked: "What did he reveal before he lost consciousness?"

"That he was dying happy, because a god was born today. He didn't speak too clearly, it was an indistinct murmur. I had to kneel and place my ear to his mouth. I'm becoming too deaf to hear the oracles."

Tiberius arose, adjusted Marcus Sempronius's mantle on his shoulders, and approached the suspended slave. With the tip of his nail he lightly ran his finger down his back, which quivered and tensed.

"Marcus Sempronius, help me get him down."

The tribune sat up, looking at the emperor in surprise. It was all so strange.

"Help me unfasten him, Marcus Sempronius, I want him to live."

More surprised still, the other stood up and said: "But Tiberius, if you desire that a god be born, you must let him die."

The emperor did not answer. Then the two of them, lifting

the rigid and yet in parts flaccid body, removed from the iron rod the hook attached to the rope around his legs and succeeded in laying him down, awkwardly, on the couch nearby. Tiberius, tearing a strip from his tunic, tied a bandage around his neck. Marcus Sempronius was following the emperor's movements: picking up an amphora, filling a cup with wine, pouring it into the half-opened mouth, and leaning forward over the protruding and glassy eyes.

"Marcus Sempronius. . . ."

He bent down to the slave, moved Tiberius aside with a gesture, leaned over, placed his ear on the rigid, motionless chest and listened. He then walked to a nearby table and took a mirror of polished metal which he placed next to the slave's half-opened mouth, and waited.

"Caesar Augustus, he is dead."


## III

Marcus Sempronius reflected on the emperors he had known intimately: the great Tiberius, whom he thought of with longing; Caligula, who had imagined he could be Tiberius; Claudius, who trembled at the thought of being emperor, and now this petulant one, whose life (it was evident, for even he, Marcus Sempronius, conspired) was only hanging by a thread. In his villa, contemplating his grandchildren who played in the shade of the trellised grapevine, looked after by an aged slave (what stories he knew, what a musician, what lessons in rhetoric he gave to the children!), Marcus Sempronius did not complain (ah, no) about life. He complained, rather, of the pains that would not leave him, not even in the tranquil dryness of the flower-covered hillsides. His wife had died (the tomb he'd had constructed was one of the most admired curiosities on the Appian Way), his daughters were married (these children belonged to one of them), his two sons lived far away, one in

Bithynia, the other in the province of Tarragon, both of them magistrates, both married and happy. His scientific pronouncements on the rigidity of bodies, and the distribution of sanguineous humors, had earned for him the respect of the learned in the Empire, for everyone knew of the opportunities he had had to conduct experiments. Held in equally high esteem was his "Apologia of Tiberius," of which Nero had ordered a special edition made for distribution to the civil servants (poor fellow, convinced that by comparison he would be justified).

Seated on the stone bench at the edge of the lake, Marcus Sempronius watched the sunset which reddened the leaves of the trellised grapevine and cast a purplish hue on the nearly ripe grape clusters. As he watched the sunset, the laughter of the children was soft music to him, underscoring the close of evening, with the distant cries of shepherds, the bleating of sheep, the tinkling of bells, the conversations of the slaves on the patio of the kitchen.

Along the sandy pathway, a slave came running in his direction. It was the Iberian his son had sent him. Marcus Sempronius felt a sudden panic grip him, an uneasiness, an anguish, a fearful inquisitiveness. Had Nero been toppled? Had he involved him in one of the many conspiracies he uncovered daily? Or was he calling on him, once more, to counsel him in the persecution of that absurd sect which engaged in all the provocations necessary to be persecuted and clandestine?

Marcus Sempronius looked at his young secretary, in whom he reposed (did he not?) the greatest confidence, to the point of forgiving innumerable faults, eccentricities, coarseness. Athis (it was the name he'd given him) stopped next to his master and said: "Marcus Sempronius, there's a man here looking for you who says he's an old friend of yours, but I've never seen him. He's asking to speak with you."

Marcus Sempronius thought that Athis, as always, was being overly dramatic, in an attempt to appear more important.

"All my old friends have already died," and he smiled. "Where does he know me from? Did he say?"

"From Judea and from Syria. He says you and he were friends when you were praetor of Antioch."

"Antioch?" And Marcus Sempronius rose, calling up with some difficulty the elegance that was still his. "Athis, what does he look like? A tall man, dark, with a black beard, eyes like fire, who's incapable of standing still?"

"He's tall and dark, and has eyes like fire. But his beard is gray and I've never seen anyone as calm, except my master Marcus Sempronius."

Marcus Sempronius, giving Athis's shoulder a slap, declared: "It can only be Saul. Tell him to enter."

"Enter where? Out here?"

"The library. And while I'm getting ready, serve him some of that special Salerno. How he enjoyed Salerno!"

And, following after Athis, who was running, Marcus Sempronius, leaning on his cane, walked to the house. Moments later, washed and perfumed, and dressed in impeccable white clothes, he approached the door to the library and, carefully raising his legs in order to avoid bumping into a series of books spread about the floor, which were the sign of his intellectual life, drew near to the figure who, with his back turned, was examining a scroll drawn from the shelf containing the poets.

Marcus Sempronius paused and said: "You've as good a nose as ever," and already the figure was turning abruptly, papyrus in hand, and they advanced, arms outstretched, toward each other, while he concluded: "It's a Greek manuscript." And they were still embraced, in a certain conventional effusiveness, when he explained: "They're poems attributed to Plato, but I think they're false."

They remained face to face then, observing one another. And the visitor, with a soft and firm voice, said:

"All philosophy is false, Marcus Sempronius."

Marcus Sempronius gestured and they both sat down, and

Saul laid the roll of papyrus on the table on which a pitcher and cups glistened.

"It's been so many years! What are you doing in Rome?" asked Marcus Sempronius. "I never heard what became of you. . . . What have you been doing?"

"Nothing of what I should be. But I'm in Rome to serve the cause of justice and of liberty."

"Nero is a monster, to be sure. I wouldn't have imagined, however, that it was necessary to come from Syria to conspire in Rome, Saul. . . . The trouble here is precisely that we have too many conspirators."

"I'm well aware of that, but for us the situation is very grave. And it was for this reason that I sought you out, and ran the risk of placing both you and me in jeopardy."

"Why?"

"Because, Marcus Sempronius, I, by the grace of God, am one of the leaders of those Christians you persecute."

Marcus Sempronius looked at him, stupefied: "You, Saul?"

"Yes."

"Is that possible? Are there Christians of your distinction? And, when someone of your distinction becomes a Christian, can he become a Christian of distinction?"

"I never had, nor do I now have any claim to distinction, Marcus Sempronius."

"But you laughed at them, Saul, I remember."

"Yes, I did. It happens, however, that I didn't know what I was doing, and every day I crucified the Lord within myself."

Marcus Sempronius stopped talking and in the library there lingered a silence through which could be heard, in the twilight that brought shadows to all corners, the muffled sounds of domestic life in the villa. It was Saul who broke the silence.

"Marcus Sempronius, the persecution must stop."

"What persecution? You know very well that your friends tried to burn Rome. Were you the one who ordered it?"

"No, I didn't. That's why I'm here. It's all a monstrous

mistake that must be set right. There are always those who, in their zeal, believe that by destroying Rome, that debauched Rome, that sinful Rome, they are carrying out the designs of God. But only one debauched and sinful Rome must be destroyed through prayer and humility: the one that corrodes our own hearts. I never spoke of any other. And when you, Romans of Rome, persecute us, you merely encourage a love of martyrdom, which, one day, will become a love of persecution. My master said: 'Love one another.' It is through love that the Lord recognizes us and we him. I've come to ask you to use your influence, which is considerable, to halt at its outset this chain of errors. So that Rome won't become the Neros who govern her, nor the Christians become the Neros who will yet govern her."

Marcus Sempronius remained pensive, and then his eyes rested on the visitor's dark face with its slender long nose, the gray beard, and finally the eyes, still as fiery as ever: "But Saul, I have, and this is the truth, no influence whatsoever. At this point, nobody has. Nor do I believe, pardon me for saying it, that the Christians will ever govern Rome."

"They will govern the world, Marcus Sempronius. And they will enlarge it beyond the Hesperides, for the greater glory of God."

"I'm remembering our conversations in Antioch. The enthusiasm with which you carried on the discussions till all hours of the night. Saul, you've transferred your impassioned enthusiasm to this religion. In those days all philosophies were true for you, while I felt none was true. And today, when I find that philosophy alone may be true, ah, a philosophy that even I don't know which it is, you believe that none can be true and that the Christians will one day rule the earth. . . . Who knows what the fates have in store? But Rome is so implacable, Saul, that neither we nor our grandchildren will ever see such a thing."

"But, if you have grandchildren, Marcus Sempronius, think of them."

"If I think of them too much, Saul, they're the ones who will not think of me. But what would you have me do? What can I do for you, and only for you, since your Christians, as I understand it, are not content to be yours?"

"Nor should they be content. Man is saved or lost on an individual basis. God grants them but one soul, and his infinite love, and the precepts that they should understand with their hearts. I always insist on this in everything I write."

"Are those your writings that circulate about, announcing that the Kingdom of God is near? And recounting stories of miracles?"

"Not all of them. And because the Spirit whispers only where it listeth, I am unable to tell you, nor would I wish to tell you, which are mine."

Marcus Sempronius smiled: "As I said, you've retained something of the philosopher you once were. But what did you think I could do for you? And, I repeat, if I am able to do anything, which I don't believe, I will do it for you only in token of our old friendship."

Once again he fixed his gaze on those luminous and profound eyes, and a troubling thought ran through him.

"But I don't know if you can still be the same friend to me that you were. You must have heard horror stories about me. My fame preceded me in Antioch. If I've changed greatly, if no one remembers any longer what after more than forty years of Empire has become common knowledge, surely I can be nothing for you but one of those corrupt Romes, one of those hearts that no amount of fire could ever purify."

"How mistaken you are, Marcus Sempronius! You don't know the infinite love of the Lord, the power that he has over Nature. No man can boast of not being precious in the sight of God. And you yourself, merely by speaking of it, have just confessed precisely that."

Marcus Sempronius knitted his brow and let out a lighthearted laugh, while resting his hands with amused firmness on his knobby knees.

"Saul, the best way I can be of help to you is not for you to begin trying to convert me."

Saul arose and walked a few paces across the room, busied himself at the shelves and, crossing his arms while leaning against one of them, looked at Marcus Sempronius and said: "I don't intend to. Nevertheless, don't forget, we only seek that which, deep in our hearts, we have already found."

Marcus Sempronius coughed dryly.

"Saul, I'm going to tell you something. You spoke of the power of your God over Nature. I'd like to believe that your God is similar to the divine essence of the Alexandrians you once esteemed so highly. But it does not matter. Besides, your Christians, most of whom are slaves from all corners of the Empire, aren't likely to be conversant with Alexandrianisms, as you were. You remember that some forty years ago or more I was— during his voluntary exile—the faithful companion of the Emperor Tiberius, may the gods preserve him in their holy glory. One night, and I've never told this to anyone, not even on that occasion to Tiberius, a fisherman came to tell me that other fishermen had heard a voice in the night, announcing the death of the god Pan. A dearly beloved slave, while being drained of his life's blood, announced to the emperor before dying—oh, those were practices we carried out then—that he died happy because a god had been born. Both these facts occurred on the same night, an overcast night in which nothing could be seen. I don't believe in portents. Do you think these two things are connected? When was that man born whom the Christians consider a god, a mortal god?"

"You say this happened forty years ago. At about that time he must have begun preaching the Word of his Father. It doesn't appear that that night coincides with his birth, which was more than twenty years before, nor with his death on the cross, a few years later."

"Tiberius later ordered some secret inquiries to be made throughout the Empire. The story of the death of Pan was gathered from the most distant outposts. The story of the birth of a god was not. Or was not, precisely because it was even more commonplace, since everyone, if we ask them, believes there is always a god being born. Do you suppose that that slave was a Christian? He was so young, he had come to Rome almost as a child, you say that your Master began to preach at that time, it's not possible."

Saul leaned away from the shelf, came over and stopped before Marcus Sempronius, who raised his hooded and vacant eyes.

"Marcus Sempronius, have you always thought about this or did you only remember it now, while speaking to me?"

"To tell you the truth, I don't know."

"Because it is possible."

"Possible?"

"Yes. Imagine that it was at the hour when he recognized his mission within himself, and felt within himself that he was the son of God and was himself God. Wouldn't that be, therefore, the very hour when my divine Master was born again, for the second time, in the full integrity of his Being? And at the moment when God, He, and the Word became one, one and indivisible, in his consciousness, wasn't that when the god Pan died?"

They could barely see one another. And they both remained silent and still, until a slave entered with a lamp which he placed on the table. The pitcher glistened. The slave slipped out as quietly as he had entered.

Marcus Sempronius arose and asked: "Will you be returning to Rome tonight? Will you stay and dine with me?"

Saul answered: "I'll be returning."

"Well, did you at least drink some of that Salerno wine I had served for you? You used to enjoy Salerno so very much."

"I did not drink any."

"Then let us drink a cup together."

He went to the table, filled two cups and extended one to Saul. Saul grasped it and they both, cups in hand, were illuminated by the yellowish glow of the lamp.

Saul spoke: "Did you know, Marcus Sempronius, that the sanctified wine is the blood of my Master?"

Marcus Sempronius thought: Tiberius used to drink the blood of slaves, but he only said: "No, I did not know." And he raised his cup: "May the gods, all the gods, be propitious unto us."

"May the Lord protect you."

They drank and set down their cups.

"Saul, in all truthfulness, I have no influence whatsoever. But I shall do what I can."

As they walked toward the door, they stumbled on the scrolls lying on the floor.

"Saul, if you are arrested, I won't allow them to torture you, to crucify you. After all, you are a Roman citizen. They can only behead you."

"In that regard, I would not invoke my Roman citizenship, which my Master did not have, for I, in my insignificant humanity, am not greater than he. But I thank you, because, as the least of his disciples, I am unworthy of the cross on which he died."

"I'll not have influence to do more."

"It is too much even so. It is everything. May God bless you."

Marcus Sempronius did not see him leave.

1961        *Translated by Frederick G. Williams*

# The Great Secret

There you will reveal to me
the things my soul desired.
*St. John of the Cross,* The Spiritual Canticle

SHE closed the door of the cell behind her and stood still, leaning against the door, feeling through her veil the hard wood against the nape of her neck. The light of the oil lamp in the oratory flickered slowly, at times crackling, and cast off a brightness in which she recognized, rather than saw, the table next to the window, with the books resting on it, the *prie-dieu,* the cot made of planks, and the worn flagstones. She knew perfectly what was awaiting her. She had felt clearly, as she got up from supper, and afterwards in the church during the prayers, that once again she would suffer the visit. . . . Just as her body refused to detach itself from the door and stand un-aided in the cell, so also, mentally, words refused to name the horror that awaited her. She shuddered: her skin, like her memory, drew back in an anxious throbbing, from which her hands were already rising in a gesture of aversion. It was all beyond her strength; she could no longer bear it. She yearned to cry for help, roll on the floor, flee through the corridors and into the open country outside. Anything would be preferable. To be assaulted a thousand times by beggars and lepers, to be brutally violated a thousand times by soldiers and bandits, to be sold a thousand times as a slave. A thousand times the repetition of all that she had known in her former life. A thousand times to live through the misfortune that this life had been until, like a refuge reached at last at the price of such misery, there had opened before her and then closed over her the doors of the monastery. When finally she entered it, she had leaned, even as now, against the door, not taking leave of the world, but feeling that everything had remained there outside, and she would be reborn, would at last experience the resurrection of her life that the weight of an immense stone, which was her destiny, had not allowed to rise and go forth. But there within, and within the resurrection, awaited the unnamable horror of being chosen, being visited, being loved more than is possible.

She shook her head from side to side. No. No. For pity's sake, no. The dreadful pains she had suffered at being violently possessed by a monster of incredible dimensions were nothing in comparison with what, in these moments, passed through her spirit. And yet the similarity was great, was so great, was too much.

When the glare began to appear between the window and the oratory, she shut fast her eyes, slipped down the length of the door, grasped her rosary and went through the beads which fled from her. It was not a temptation that she repelled in this way; but it was, as she well knew, an effort to satisfy the heavens with the spiritual offering of a prayer. And yet everything in her tormented body affirmed that it would be useless. The glare increased, as always, and, as always, even with eyes closed she could trace the scent of the luminous immensity which effaced the walls of the cell, wrapping her in a tepid tenderness that hurt her to the quick. The soft music, too, hurt her; and yet this music, which she sensed without hearing, did not mingle with the brightness. It was rather an accompaniment, a background against which the light grew greater and wider. Before long the voices would come, pressing every recess of her body, like fiery pincers or like lips, leeches, tongues.

In a painful effort, she opened her eyes. The brightness filled the entire cell, and the cot, the oratory, the books, the *prie-dieu*, the table, the flagstones, the portals of the windows, even the oil lamp itself—all hovered in a cadenced undulation, in a weightless whirl, and sailed as if with full sails while splendorous wakes whispered of all things as if along the hull of a ship.

Now it was her habit and veil, the hairshirt that she wore about her waist, and the rosary that very slowly rose up and joined the gentle saraband. The suffocating and lacerating brutality was already penetrating her, while weakness crushed her very bowels and bones. Everything within her opened and fragmented, thousands of needles pricked her, knives tore her, columns filled her, waterfalls drowned her, flames burned over luminous, singing waters and alighted like will-o'-the-wisps all along her body.

Contracting herself into a final refusal, but at the same time yielding that it might all end, she was deluged by a crystalline ardor which spread out faintly from her core, there where the Presence, filling her, pounded at the dissolving boundaries of her flesh. The light reached an unbearable brilliance; the music thundered over everything; she felt herself bathed viscously in shouts and cries that bit her. . . . And in the sudden silent darkness she felt, on her back, on the nape of her neck and on her legs, the cold and violent hardness of the flagstones on which she had fallen.

She opened her eyes in the darkness. Her pained and disarrayed body, the cold and the lamp that glowed flickering, reminded her that she had entered her cell; but with vehemence, horror, rebellious humility, she remembered nothing else. She let herself remain stretched out, savoring a discomfort that was to her an exhausted repose. And she began to hear the murmur of the prayers, the voice of the Mother Abbess, mutterings that detached themselves and that she came to recognize.

Light raps sounded on the door, the latch clicked, and the Abbess and two others entered, silhouetted in the diffuse glare that came from the corridor, where the prayers continued. She saw their habits close to her face, the folds rising up and disappearing into the darkness. They had come, as always, to listen, jealous of the favors heaped upon her, compassionate of the suffering that fell to her lot, fascinated and frightened, praying that they might help her and might also share in that resonant brightness that flowed out through the cracks in the door. When they thus bent over her and lifted her, and tenderly laid her on the cot and remained on their knees, filling the cell and the corridor, praying with her, they could not imagine the great shame that tortured her, now different, now the same as the shame she had felt when the emir, in the center of the tent, had ordered that she be undressed and that the soldiers, one after the other, possess her in public. She had refused to take part in his harem, as first wife, and he, who prized and preferred her and had purchased her from pirates and had brought her there with exquisite refinement, had ordered the eunuchs to stretch her out on the divan and hold her.

Lying on the cot with eyes closed, she extinguished all recollections from her memory. She felt herself slowly descending into a dark and humid bottomless pool. Neither the presence of the others nor their voices had any power against the solitude and the silence. This was the moment that, in the end, she most feared. It was in these moments that, she well knew, she consented to the next visit, yielded in advance to the call and to the light, whenever they would come. On the following day, at dawn, after a stony sleep, it would all have passed. The other sisters would cross her path, greeting her with deference, offering or attempting to offer a compassionate look, a friendly smile. The Abbess would call her to talk about current matters, news of the armies and of relatives, of battles in Jersualem, and of the Holy Sepulcher. And suddenly, in the cell, cloister, garden, or cellar, when she would be alone, even tomorrow or a month from now, by day or by night, it would all be repeated and would begin again. For invariably, whatever they did, there were moments when the others would go away from her, leaving her alone, as it to propitiate the repetition of events that were the honor of the convent. And great lords or poor beggars would come and try to see her, through the grille of the choir, or ask that she touch them. The Abbess would drag her off, eyes closed, would grasp her hand and slip it through the grille, and she would feel their tears and their drooling kisses on it. The Abbess herself, leading her back in silence to the cloister, would clean her hand.

She drew to her bosom the hand that was hanging over the cot, and now they were kissing her. She sighed. Within her closed eyes she saw the crucifix that was in the church in her native land, so long ago, so far away, on the borders of Europe. A strange amazement went quavering through her from head to toe. Never again had she seen it, nor had she remembered it sight unseen, nor even had there passed through her spirit the memory, unrecognized, of remembering it. The image smiled at her and then she, a girl looking around to make sure she was alone, had raised her hand to the sendal that girded him, and had tried to lift it to have a look. For *he* could not fail to be like other men. But the sendal, which seemed a fine light silk, was sculpted in wood, and she had sadly lowered her hand, feeling that her curiosity had been punished.

She opened her eyes and saw that she was alone. A peace, tranquillity, satiation which was not in her but in the air that surrounded her, released the last contractions from her bruised body. Still she felt, but very far off, pains that were scattered, or concentrated where the violence had been greatest. But the well-being was enormous and molded her lips into a smile.

The great secret, now she knew the great secret. And she fell asleep.

The glare again began to fill the cell, but now it neither increased nor resounded. Rather, it remained about her like a canopy, an attentive and watchful tenderness that, leaning down, contemplated her, so crushed and suffering, breathing peacefully.

1961                                    *Translated by Daphne Patai*

# A Very Brief Tale

A tale must be brief.
*Several authors**

*T*HIS is a brief tale. It is, indeed, very brief. Moreover, if it were not brief, extremely brief, it would risk not being a tale at all. Tales, more than men, are obliged above all to recognize their limits.

Intending as I do to write a brief tale, as brief as this one, it is impossible for me to say anything about myself. Brevity does not allow those elaborations, almost always vanity, in which we sacrifice a narrative in the interest of our selves. Now, if there is anything I hate to sacrifice, even in my own self-interest, it's a narrative.

Of course to narrate, as everybody knows, is not sufficient to write a tale. But neither, as all will acknowledge, is it an absolute necessity: besides, if the tale is brief, very brief, the space for narrative is so diminished that it scarcely fits; and, were we to force the narrative, it would, just like the intrusion of our persons, extend the limits—those very limits which one must recognize—beyond what is reasonable in a brief tale.

For, let's face it, brevity is everything. Brevity allows for prudence, restraint, reserve, modesty. Modesty is essentially a brief virtue.

*In English in the original (Ed.).

Without doubt, however, virtues, even brief ones, are precluded by the brevity of a very brief tale. Aside from which it is a firm and proven point that virtues as such are entirely alien to literary aesthetics. And a brief tale is, above all, a work of art, of literary art, where everything boils down to artistic effect.

Nevertheless, in the brevity of a tale it is extremely difficult, if not impossible, to prepare for an effect. If we do not wish, and I do not, merely to relate an anecdote, reasonable limits do not allow for such preparatives. The latter, like the loss of virtues, requires preparation, although the loss itself might be practically instantaneous, whether it be felt in the moment in which it is lost (virtue), or whether it be a later discovery, when someone discovers he is missing something ("thing" is a manner of speaking) that had after all been lost. In a brief tale it is as doubtful that there be room for virtues as it is doubtful that they might be lost.

I remember that once, in London, I was standing on a corner looking for the post office that was somewhere nearby. I had inquired, and it was somewhere nearby. Then an elderly lady, with steel-framed spectacles and an enormous kale protruding from a string bag, stopped at my side, turned to me, pushed aside her grizzled and dirty hair that was drooping from beneath a pointed but shapeless black felt hat, and asked me where the post office was. Immediately my eyes, after having stared at the ash-gray overcoat and flat shoes with their great buckles that made up the rest of her image, searched the buildings—all Georgian with white windows set in walls of another tone of white—and found the post office. I pointed it out to her, and the woman thanked me effusively and crossed the street. While she was crossing, I took a few steps along the sidewalk, and saw, displayed in a shop window, a porcelain Chinaman covered with dust. And, suddenly, I turned back, because—I realized—I had no letter to post (there was a letter box next to me) and I did not wish to purchase stamps (I had stamps in my pocket).

I cannot forget the brevity of this episode, not because it is an episode, which it's not, nor even because I am or am not certain of the reason why I can't forget it. It has occurred to me that this could have something to do with the picture I saw in the paper, I don't know if it was the following day, of an old woman murdered in a post office. But, if I remember correctly, the post office was in another neighborhood. Still, it's probable that the reason (for my being or not being certain) lies merely in its brevity, an insignificant, insignificative brevity, completely without content, like modesty, so essentially brief.

But, upon more careful reflection, perhaps brevity does not excuse the lack of concentration which has made me ever unable to capitalize upon an accident. Though it might be due to my natural (and previously mentioned) hesitation in perceiving, in this accident, an incident. It is a distinction of the greatest importance if one is to recognize limits. And limits, which it is so imperative to recognize, limits alone, and nothing else, allow us to make definitions. Without definitions, brevity does not exist, it is not realized, in the same way that, with definitions, brevity has neither an essence of its own nor any virtual structure. And a brief—very brief—tale that may be the actual abandonment of narrative (and to narrate implies, let us note, to interpret or, at least, to choose), and in which we may pass incognito (although not outside of time and space), being nothing more, will in all certainty be brevity unexpected, brevity captured, brevity in itself, all the more since, in the present case, I never saw that old woman again, though (unless she was the one in the photograph) I might have passed her in the street on other occasions. Not many, given this hypothesis, because I left soon after that (I cannot guarantee that it was precisely soon) for Belgium. But brevity exempts us from all dangers. Now dangers are, almost always, quite brief indeed. In view of which we can all agree that the present tale is very brief.

1961                          *Translated by Carolyn Richmond*

# Defense and Justification of a Former War Criminal

*( from the memoirs of Herr Werner Stupnein,
former high official of the SS )*

> Afraid? Of whom am I afraid?
> *Emily Dickinson*

*L*IUBLIONOVGRAD was a wretched town on the borders
of the Ukraine, completely unworthy of my standing as a high
official of the SS. My assignment to that post was the result of
ridiculous rivalries, in which, although right was on my side, I
did not carry the day. I had always been a competent and dedicated officer, the purity of my blood was above any suspicion,
and I had never had secret passions for Jewish women or Jewish
boys—something not all my superiors, or my rival, could boast
of. Although I never opened my mouth, not even to an intimate
friend, to reveal what I knew about those men who were pro-
moted, decorated, awarded honors, and despite there having
never—I'm certain of this—passed through my eyes, in their
presence, a glimmer of irony or superiority, they apparently felt
and ridiculed my erudition. For my cultural interests were vast
and my anxiety enormous to put them at the service of the only
thing capable of giving them meaning: the victory of the Germanic spirit, the imperishable dominion of the German people

over the Universe. Now that it's all over, I can acknowledge what I always knew: how insufficient, without his magical presence, were the Führer's teachings. What a cheap philosophy for such a great destiny! Yet the truth is that if it had been more costly, it would not have inflamed, as it did inflame, so many idiots inferior to me. I, in fact, accepted it by an act of intelligence, recognizing it and measuring it by the importance that distinguished it, and, like few others, developing it to the extreme limits—which it failed to attain—of logical dignity.

If before the war Liublionovgrad was a small rural town, forgotten but prosperous (if the word prosperity can have meaning where it is not the future of the German race that conditions and defines it), when I arrived there to establish my regional command, it was nothing more than a hamlet in ruins. The Russians, in their retreat, had taken almost everything, and the German armies, crossing through it in glorious pursuit, had taken the rest. However carefully I inspected the entire town, as was my duty, house by house, well by well, I could find nothing of artistic value other than one beautiful icon, superbly framed in gold, hanging behind the door of a house. I still have this icon, which, in its barbarous primitivism, must date from the sixteenth century—when German art attained such high splendor—and it perfectly reflects, in the absurd stylization of the figures (a Virgin with her Son in her lap), in the gilded background, in the firm lines and colors, the congenital deformities of the Slavic soul. The frame I remitted to the Reich's Treasury, although I could have taken it apart and kept it, as everyone used to do whenever it was possible to benevolently appropriate the spoils of war. When I assumed the command whose headquarters were, incomprehensibly, in that lost village (which, without doubt, the General Staff had chosen through an error in the size of the letters of the map), its inhabitants had already returned to their homes, if we can apply the word "home" to those houses made of wood, occupied by Communists or their slaves. Moreover, the inhabitants who had returned were only old men, women, and children. Among these frightened and silent people, who never seemed to see me when I passed in the street, the male sex was represented merely by those who were not yet men or who, for all purposes, had already ceased to be men. Even the women: it was hard to find one who was still in the prime of life, who was pretty, appetizing, with that merry and rosy vigor that makes country girls so resemble ripe apples. It was clear that the inhabitants, for the most part, had not returned of their own free will. When I established my command, my men were forced to make systematic raids in the vicinity and even some distance from the village, raids that the rear guard on the march had already begun, to flush out people who had idiotically hidden in the woods. But many, beset by hunger and by bad weather, or even—if it's possible—by the habit of living in their houses (although the houses were certainly not theirs, since property was not recognized and protected there, as it was so rigorously in the Third Reich), had appeared hesitant and fearful, at the outskirts of the town, where the sentries found them, or, to such a point do these yokels sneak about like animals, had turned up from one day to the next at the doors or windows of houses still abandoned the previous evening.

These were, as a matter of fact, the problems I had to resolve first, still embittered by the solitude of those borders, where there was not a soul with whom I might share my cultural ruminations. My library, not my Berlin library but a small selection from it that had accompanied me through various relocations in the service of the Reich, never managed to reach me, though I had left it packed with the greatest care. In its place, and as if they were my books, there arrived one day a truck loaded with packing crates of the sort described in numerous shipping and transport handbooks and which, puzzled, I ordered opened. Inside were copies of *Mein Kampf,* editions of the Führer's speeches, works by Rosenberg and other writers such as Jünger (whom I admired), all in German. Why should I want all of that, instead of my beloved companions, my books? And what was I to do with that pile of books? Distribute them to the peasants, who were illiterate, or who, even if they weren't, could read only Russian—itself a form of illiteracy? In my disappointment, foreseeable at once given the number of crates, at my books' disappearance, at their having landed in the hands of some idiot commandant, in straits similar to those in which I found myself, in this disappointment I felt the craving to return them all, and to complain. But who could guarantee to me that both this consignment and the substituted crates were not acts malignantly contrived by my enemies to cause my downfall? So the crates remained, and in a public square I solemnly conducted a distribution—duly registered in a ledger, with the names of the recipients—to the troops, to my administrative staff, and to the population at large. And I submitted a copy of that ledger, as well as of my speech on that occasion, to my hierarchical superiors, lauding my initiative and even calling their attention to the fact that my staff had shown such interest that the supply of books had been completely depleted and it had not been possible to fill all the requests. Calculatedly, I did not ask for another consignment, so as to sound out their intentions.

But the problems I had first to resolve were in fact other. The forced or voluntary return of the town's inhabitants had raised grave questions, given that many houses were occupied by my personnel; and it was obvious that Germans could not be dispossessed by members of an inferior race, subjects of a defeated country which was the greatest natural enemy of the Reich. Apart from which I did not know who among my subordinates were informers of the Gestapo, charged with spying on my activities. Therefore, following express instructions for such cases (and it is very easy, on paper, to resolve everything down to the last particular), I prescribed that the Ukrainian familes were to resume possession of their houses, after an inquiry among the population concerning the veracity of their claims, and that the new German dwellers would assume, within these houses, the position of occupants, that is, occupying the rooms they considered necessary for their lodgings, up to a maximum limit of all the rooms minus one, and receiving from the *de jure* dwellers, since they were the *de facto* ones, the performance of domestic services.

The absence of women in the prime of life or of a nubile age was, however, a much more complicated case. Doubtless it eliminated one of my greatest concerns as a conscientious and reliable administrator, sparing me from having to be on guard to eliminate annoying cases of carnal weakness between an occupier and an occupied so far apart on the human ladder, cases such as the establishment of continuous relations, attachments of a permanent character, passions fed by isolation and by physical necessities. But without a doubt it also made it difficult for me to find a solution, according to the norms, for the physical satisfactions required by the large number of men who were my subordinates. One of the concerns of my superiors was to recommend or order the installation of brothels, utilizing the available women as raw material. For, aside from copulations eugenically destined for the production and propagation of a superior and purified race, German morality quite rightly did not permit our young German women to constitute an auxiliary corps within the Army—unlike the Americans who aimed at the hypocritical satisfaction of a natural necessity through inconceivable romances between officers. Indeed, it is not logical, nor does it aid in the maintenance of hierarchical respect, for a lieutenant to conquer the favors of a major, even when this major is an attractive woman. For some time I dedicated the best part of my attention to this problem, which even surfaced in several cases that I had to suppress with tolerance and understanding (precisely because they occurred in the person of beings devoid of human attributes or civilization), involving collective rapes of old women or of children of both sexes. As far as I was concerned, the problem did not exist, for I have always known how to discipline my imagination. But I understood that not everyone had the same intellectual discipline that I had perfected. How many absurd and abstract orders, exhibiting no knowledge of reality, did I receive! How many reports did I send, trying to open the eyes of those theorists! Until I discovered, all by myself, the logical and rational solution to this momentous question, which I disclosed in a pamphlet. This pamphlet, printed by order of the highest authorities, enjoyed widespread official propagation, despite the envious opposition of many of my chiefs. In it I demonstrated, along with practical experience, my years of reflection on German ethics.

Evidently there does not exist any natural morality, valid for all beings. And it is equally evident that morality is not, as the Marxists would have it, a class prejudice. Morality is the mass of practical rules elaborated through the experience of the species in its selective struggle for survival and domination. Within this order of ideas, scientifically demonstrable and demonstrated, it is reasonable to eliminate any elements contrary to the progressive evolution of the human species, represented by German destiny, and it is a crime for a German to injure another pure German who, like himself, has an equal right to contribute to and participate in this progress. From the Christian point of view, this vision of the world attributes to all human beings an individual soul, which has its roots in the absurdity of supposing that an insurmountable difference exists between animals and man. The difference is, in fact, a difference in *quality,* but this quality, as is biologically so clear, does not have individual characteristics. A people is not a summation of individuals united by the same interests. Quite the contrary, what creates and develops individuals is the acceptance of interests that the people, in their ever more conscious activity of biological ascension, attribute to them. The German people are not a mass of pure Germans. The Germans, rather, are purifying themselves as they acknowledge this superior mission which defines and identifies the German people. If this is so, what may well be a crime among Germans takes on a completely different meaning when creatures of other races are involved. It is unthinkable, for example, for a German woman to be a prostitute, or that various Germans could, on this basis, have relations with her. But it is perfectly understandable and justifiable that a woman of an inferior race be one. Doubtless the bourgeois and Christian criterion of remuneration is what actually defines the prostitute; and this remuneration, despite everything, is what constitutes acknowledgment of equality, for it is the payment for a service rendered. Just as we do not individually remunerate the chickens we eat (and this is the idiotic argument of vegetarians, as if vegetables did not also partake of the world soul which is Life), so an inferior race *has no right* to remuneration. It cannot, in the biological panorama, be more than a utility. Now, if this is so, every type of relation with such a woman is not only justified, but legitimate. This is true to such an extent that, in Western Christian bourgeois society based on a customary or legally enforced stratification of classes (with which the purely German origin of institutions was betrayed), and not based on the unity of a differentiated people, "vices" are in fact only considered "vices" when practiced between individuals of different classes. As long as a person does not, through sheer dastardliness, go beyond the limits of his class, conniving with a lower class on an equal commercial footing; or as long as, out of a spirit of prostitution (and thus is class "dignity" defended), he limits himself to having relations with individuals of a higher class, in no way whatsoever is he considered, by his equals, "corrupted" or "reprobate." If this is how it is in a class society, which posits a pretended equality among human beings independently of race, there can rest no shadow of a doubt that in a society such as the German, in which biological truth is restored to its proper terms, these questions pose themselves in an altogether inverse way, and one can only consider nefarious whatever goes on among the individuals of a superior race, particularly that race which, in its bosom, is enacting a process that under the Führer's direction leads it away from pure animality. And what would be, among Germans, abnormal and bestial (due also to the danger of contaminating oneself with affective elements that would remove the character of pure play or pure camaraderie from these relations), as it is when practiced by inferior individuals racially submerged in the animal state (with the difference that, in this state, as when we accept the behavior of cats and dogs, the ethical question does not arise, for it appears only as one passes from the state of "species" to the state of "people"), ceases completely to be abnormal and bestial when practiced between Germans and individuals of other races. And thus it is that rape, homosexuality, sadism, etc., are perfectly legitimate in these circumstances. To raise, for example, doubts about passive pederasty or masochism, does not follow, inasmuch as in none of these cases is the pleasure of the active agent in question, for he merely plays a role which is demanded of him or determined by an element that is biologically superior to him.

These ideas of mine, above all regarding sexuality, caused an enormous scandal among those personalities still leashed to the monstrous traditions of irrational moralism. Public discussion of my pamphlet—in which I carefully developed and extended my argumentation with the greatest scientific objectivity, relying on citations from the best biological, ethnological, and sociological sources—was actually forbidden. But it was nonetheless widely distributed and many of my conclusions were used in circulars and in various publications. What still pains my conscience today, and causes me to express my greatest revulsion, is the rationale for which this was done. Once again and always, it was the anti-national-socialist substrata who acted and agitated. My ideas were propagated not because they were logical and reasonable, but because they contributed to the depravation and degradation of the inferior races! As if, from the biological and philosophical perspective, this depravation and degradation were possible! Depravation is a concept resulting from the Christian notion of sin, and this, in turn, depends on the belief in an individual soul which can thus be led to its "perdition." But where there exists no soul, how can there be depravation? In the same way, since the spirit of the German people is collective, the exercise of so-called "vices" that have as their instrument inferior beings cannot constitute depravation. If I mistreat an animal or an inferior human being, I don't therefore deprave it: I merely commit, perhaps, an unnecessary act, which it is not if, on my part, it is a conscious and well-intentioned effort to lead him to the philosophical recognition of his place on the biological ladder. And since it is a question of biology, rational arguments are not, evidently, the ones that must, logically, be used.

I had, however, some consolations in the exercise of my administration at that time. Discreetly, with the prudence demanded by the incomprehension of the obtuse (after having, for some time, maintained a tolerance that permitted me to study, *de visu,* the behavior of human beings and of the men entrusted to my authority), I was systematically putting into practice the ideas I had expounded. The problem of women, which persisted for a great many of those who apparently remained faithful to conventional tastes—that is, those who, if on the one hand they controlled their imaginations, on the other hand had none—this problem I managed to resolve in part (nor did it interest me to resolve it to the fullest extent possible, in order to maintain the conditions necessary for my discreet experiments) by undertaking carefully organized hunts, lengthy cynegetic expeditions, which intoxicated my men and which, I confess, I liked to lead personally. I cannot forget those cavalcades (this is a manner of speaking, tainted, however, by appropriate suggestions of Antiquity, but incompatible with the semi-armored units in which they were made) through the immense steppe, the discovery of a forgotten village, an isolated cabin where, behind a stack of hay, or in a hidden cellar, or in a loft full of spiderwebs, we would find a woman still in acceptable physical condition or, more delectable fruit, a somewhat spirited young woman, at the right age to endure and contain within her the onslaught of vigorous and domineering Germans. It was on one of these occasions that, at some distance from the major part of the column, alone in my automobile with the driver and my orderly, I came upon a farmhouse which seemed totally abandoned and deserted. We entered it with submachine guns in hand, for although my zone was rather calm one always had to expect that these houses might be, at least temporarily, the hiding place of guerrillas. I never understood, let me say in passing, the obstinacy of these guerrillas. Inferior races, liberated by the German people from the tyrannical fiction of being forced to conduct themselves like men, and allowed to return, under our aegis, to their happy animal state. . . . I have never understood it, except by resorting to the notion, so important biologically, of mimicry and imitation. But to continue my recollection: we entered the house and went through it all without finding anyone. Then, just as we were leaving, a peculiar rustle in a hidden corner of the very kitchen by which we had entered revealed to us the presence of what, breaking down a small door made of planks, turned out to be, in an out-of-the-way nook, a girl of about fifteen, ragged and dirty, but with what eyes and breasts! . . .

When my two companions took hold of her, she, struggling, urinated down her legs out of foolish fright. In the rural atmosphere, with the smell of the steppe entering through the door on a light breeze, the urine trickling down added to her sharp, wild-animal charm. I did not resist, it was the only time that I did not resist. She, however, resisted; and I preserve as the best recollection of those ineffable moments the respect toward me, the delicacy, the firm decision, without any hint of morbid curiosity or libidinous promiscuity, with which my driver and orderly held her for me. The least that was demanded of me by loyalty and camaraderie among individuals of a superior race, separated only by military hierarchy, was to wait afterwards, at the door, which I did, as each of them used her while the other held her down. When the two of them reappeared (and in the tempered elegance of their manners could be seen the pure and guileless health of German youth), she, head down and tearful, with her tattered clothes reduced to almost nothing, moved between both of them, and they supported her on her feet. But in her eyes, lit by the golden, green, orange-hued sunset that was burning the steppe, there was a new gleam: such is the power of the revelation of sex, when undertaken by superior men devoid of sentimental scruples!

I think that the reputation for harmonious liberty which was enjoyed, within the strictest and most lucid observation of national-socialist ideals, in the region I commanded, echoed in Germany and even in the occupied countries. On one pretext or another, many people asked for transfers to my towns and villages, or arrived there in the performance of the most startling duties. All this required, for the preservation of the high level of my experiments, a rigorous selection on my part of the elements that were admitted, so that there would not be insinuated among them, as often happened, some individual who, through irremediable baseness, was less conscious or more forgetful of the composure demanded by Germanic ethics. At one point I had to impose discipline authoritatively. And I even found myself obliged to order, as an example, the castration in a public execution of one man—he was a Slovene, as it happens—much sought after by various less conventional elements (and let us agree that he was, although worn out, a splendid stud), who had boasted, as the investigation revealed, of the pleasure that he took, and even dared to make the most disrespectful comparisons among the individuals who required his services. One of these had been, much to my surprise, my very virile and elegant orderly. But, apart from this and the scandal, which I also had to settle, of a sadist who clearly went too far (he was going through three or four children per week, according to the Chinese method of ducks and geese, or, if you prefer, of the marshal of France, Gilles de Rais, a forerunner of genius who lacked only culture and the right historical moment), forgetting that the reserves were not unlimited and that circumstances did not permit organization of large-scale production, and forgetting also the solidarity he owed to the others interested in the same kind of gratification; apart from these I managed to administer my ideal State, to the contentment of all and of myself, despite the inevitable deficiencies caused by wartime disorganization, and despite the malicious denunciations that my enemies, the envy of my rivals, or the repressed pettiness of individuals who would have liked to be subject to my orders, never ceased to bruit about.

But in the scholarly peace of my retirement, in the bitterness of our defeat, and in the grief of seeing forgotten or scorned the pure, altruistic disinterest of my doctrines, so logical, so just and so practical (as my experience demonstrated), I am aging calmly. Nothing weighs on my conscience, which is pure; and I know that if many outdid themselves, in cowardly zeal, in the performances of their duties (or, after all, because they performed them begrudgingly), I was the arbiter of an extraordinary endeavor, of the greatest scientific and sociological scope, which only the defeat of our armies and the pressing advance of the enemy destroyed. One certainty, however, remains with me: Humanity, when it frees itself from the millennial slavery of ideals and interests contrary to the realization of its superior destiny, will recognize the merit of my ideas. Numerous indications reveal this to me. It is true that in Russian, Czech, and French tribunals, and—supreme irony—in German ones, I was judged *in absentia* and condemned. By means of various charges, these tribunals twice condemned me to death, and to prison terms amounting to one hundred two years and six months. I smile to myself when I think of this. I am alive, free, and do not even hide under an assumed name or in exile. I do not reside, it is true, in my hometown or in Berlin. But I am, as I always was, a respected citizen, and I even belong to the Town Council of the city in which I live. This, of course, is not the result—and it is a sore spot in my peace of mind, tarnished only by the loss of my library in the bombings of Berlin—of the value of my ideas, but of my having faithfully served the Reich. Besides, I was not judged for my ideas, but for my "crimes." I was always exact in my reports and in my statistics. They accused me of having personally directed the killing of 2,754 people of both sexes and various ages and races. This is completely false. I never *killed* anyone, directly or indirectly. During my administration, in varied circumstances, and in accordance with the administrative principles that the enemies of the Reich were aware of and never openly condemned, 1,893 members of the human species died. And I never prevented any of them, as adults, from whipping any German masochist who sought them out. As far as children are concerned, I have to say that, between dying uselessly of hunger or of the misfortunes of war—their natural fate—and being rationally used in the legal pleasures of an organized and superior society, it seems to me there is no dilemma. The dilemma of this world is another, and it consists in knowing if there is some natural sanction preventing the affirmation of biological supremacy. I firmly believe that there is not. This thought is shared by my friends—and even ex-enemies—scattered throughout the world, or highly placed (as I refused to be, out of repugnance at the hypocrisy of pretending to acknowledge as our equals the bloc of inferior or misled races that defeated us) in the current administration, with whom I correspond. I mentioned earlier the indications that justify my infallible hope in the final victory of my ideas. I am not referring, naturally, to that spirit of ethical indifference which, so I gather, is spreading throughout the world. Only in appearance will this cynicism lead to results analogous to those arising from my principles. I never preached liberty, but rather order; I never preached equality, but rather hierarchy; I never preached fraternity, but rather the free will of the race that purified itself in order to attain it. What our neighbor does cannot leave us indifferent, because our only reason for living is a consequence of the superior and selective meaning of Life. Democratic indifferentism blindly and criminally ignores the playful character of cruelty, one of the most innocent manifestations of the vital instinct. The child who tortures a bird, the cat who toys with the mouse—here is an ethic. The only one. And, beyond all contingencies, there is in fact an immanent biological justice of which, in the unjust humbleness of my hierarchic rank, I was the representative, at a privileged moment in History; this is what the tranquillity of my existence and the vitality of the ideals that I perfected clearly prove. Unlike others who live in despair, preoccupied with taking a stand for or against ideologies which have nothing to do with us, I will die certain and secure in the knowledge that I was one of the highest and most legitimate zeniths of human consciousness, on the path to its most authentic future.

1961                                    *Translated by Daphne Patai*

# By the Rivers of Babylon

Geniuses do not have, do not need to
have, a biography.
*Latino Coelho,* Luís de Camões,
*Lisbon, 1880*

 *T* HE ascent up the dark, narrow, and steep staircase
with its high and crooked steps was a torture whenever he
returned to the house. By dint of balancing himself, half leaning
against the wall whose whitewash had long since faded even on
his back, and supporting one of his crutches diagonally on the
farthest end of the step above, he went cautiously up, breathless
with anger at his slowness. All of the unction acquired in conversation with the friars of St. Dominic, whose prelections he
regularly attended, remaining then to confer with them, was
lost in the return home at afternoon's end. Hardly had he settled
himself to rest at the window, seated at the small low bench, his
soup eaten, ruminating memories and sadness, but his old
mother would proceed in her interminable tidying, punctuated
with beginnings of conversation to which he would respond
with smiles and distracted monosyllables or with dry phrases in
which he retorted more to himself than to her. Sometimes she
would persist, repeating a comment and awaiting his answer.
But even this persistence did not signify effective communica-
tion: she only pretended to calm her own conscience and her pity
for her aged and sick son whom life had destroyed, addressing

some words to him in a pretended conversation that would not
leave him dangerously abandoned to his solitary thoughts, into
which, as is well known, the Enemy particularly worms his way.
And it was not of the thoughts that he was afraid, but of the ever
greater spaces that occurred between the thoughts. When she
spoke to him, and above all when she persisted, he had to keep
himself from being distracted by the words he was hearing: or
soon, in the interrupted flow of ideas that continually wandered
off like an agitated river, a tenebrous void would open, a dark
vortex in which hovered shreds of verses and of things he had
seen, and, further down, something like a very small illuminated door, or a glass laid over strange waters in which rare
beings were swimming and that looked like an eye gazing at
him, blinking or pulsating, he could not tell—perhaps, yes,
not even an eye, but a watery transparency like the reflections of
waves in the moonlight. The small door, which made him
dizzy, was not always in evidence. Most of the time there was
nothing more than the pool over which he leaned, anxious for
the little door to open and tremulous to the point of shivers from
the chill that it emitted. Closing his eyes, pressing them with
some strength, he managed then to banish those visions, or that
vision, always the same one, that he dreamt awake. For he hated
the dreams. To think, to be distracted, to remember, to imagine, even to suppose how everything might have been in a
triumphant life and in another world, this was not a dream but
the certainty that he existed, that things arranged themselves
according to his wish, that their order and the World's was a
discord which he mentally organized. When he slept, he never
dreamt. They were not dreams, the things that he then saw, but
the continuation of the same power and the same certainty, or
else temptations of the devil, as the priests would say. But
temptations that he knew well. They were not temptations for
his soul, which God would never allow to be lost, unless it were
in that strange vortex where it seemed that he did not pene-

trate. Temptations, how? What temptation was it to have in his arms a woman who had escaped him? What temptation was it to kill, sleeping, a powerful and inaccessible enemy? What temptation was it to see himself happy in a palace, rich, respected, encircled by servants and admirers, with a table laden with good tidbits and good wines, and with health and energy for some games of arms or for a beautiful lover fished from the street, every day a different one? What temptation seeing himself at Court, with a good velvet doublet and a collar of fine laces, hearing the praises of his peers, and reciting or reading his latest poem? These things were not temptations, no, but merciful consolations to his soul, the satisfaction of all that had eluded him, the plenitude of what he had not had, the satiation of what had been insufficient, the conquest of what could never have been his. Sin is to dream of the future: to desire the woman seen in that instant, to want fiercely what is given to others, to envy furiously, like a thing stolen from us, another's happiness which dances, shamelessly and unconcerned with our misery, before our eyes that stop at the sight of it. But to imagine himself happy in the past, with all that had fleetingly grazed him and had never been to the measure of his hunger, this was not temptation, this was not a sin; it was, yes, his only riches, his only reason for waiting for death, dried of love, weak in enthusiasm, disbelieving in his homeland, devoid even of the joy of writing verses. His verses, now, had abandoned him. They had dissolved, like sugar, in the uninterrupted river of thought where in the past they used to bob up abruptly, like pieces of burning ice that one by one joined together to make a poem. And he did not long for them at all. It had never been for himself that he had written them. For others, yes. So that they would hear him, so that they would marvel at him, so that they would understand him, so that they would see how everything in life had a precise meaning that only he was capable of discovering, an architecture that it would not have without him, a beauty that does not exist except as the idea first thought by whoever is worthy of it.

He pushed open the door and entered. Contrary to her habit, his mother did not appear, nor did he sense in the house any noise. He closed the door, went to the table and sat down in a chair, propping up the crutches. Sitting was a relief from fatigue, and a new torture as well. But his mother's absence, so unusual, made less torturous the torture of sitting adjusting his swollen and painful parts, an act that, with infinite shame, he was obliged to perform before her, and that he therefore did not do properly, feeling the old woman's eyes fixed on his, horrified at the monstrosity of the punishments reserved for those who surrender to the sins of the flesh, who abandon the purity with which they came into the world. She who, when her husband would return from a voyage, only allowed him to kiss her after making certain he had not disembarked at any port, for many months. . . . Sighing, he smiled to himself. On the first voyage he had made, upon embarking for India, still shaken from the orgies of so many nights on end, aimed at preparing him for a long period of sky and sea and the talk of men, he . . . made the sign of the cross. These memories were temptations of the flesh. And in this lay the difference from the poetry he had written throughout his life. At times he had indeed written in order to know what he was thinking. But other times he had written in order truly to possess, as in his youth he used to repeat the act of love again and again, not because he felt desire but in order to more clearly feel that he possessed, to be certain that he really possessed the harlot whom he had forgotten the first time. Now, thus decrepit and impotent, everything that he used to think, if he were to write it, seemed to him to be but the kind of poetry that sinned against the Holy Ghost, and that was not a bestowal, an offering of his body to the body he entered, but a pillaging, an avarice, a way of devouring his fellow being. And even with all that he had written, it seemed to him uncertain that he had done it in abnegation, for he had always aspired for others' recognition, for triumph, glory, prizes, to the point of being contented with the constrained smiles of the ignorant people to whom he would read his poems.

He raised his eyes to the window. In the building opposite, he saw the caulker seated at the table, observing him amicably above his steaming wooden bowl. He motioned to him with his head, and the other man made a broad gesture with his hand and ended up pointing to the soup in a kind offer. He responded with a gesture as if of farewell, and looked away. Two children came up and leaned against the veranda; he did not need to look in order to know. He had never liked children, had never thought of taking a wife in order to have his own. Perhaps this was why so much or all of his poetry had remained like those children we did not wish to have, and who later detach themselves from us, divining a detachment that we regret but that does not cease to be detachment, even regretted. Love was, for him, flesh and spirit, so fleshly that no spirit could be present, and so spiritual that not even all the flesh in the world, used day and night, was sufficient to satisfy it. Even boredom, which at times took him far from carnal contacts, was an unsatisfied fervor, which restrained itself, suspended and threatening, waiting to forget that flesh was always the same and the gestures of love so few that he had long known them by heart. But afterwards, in repeating them, it was always, like the first time, a surprise, a curious ignorance, a timid fear, a sweet incertitude, a juvenile awe, a new joy, a frenetic enchantment; it was like the first initiation, but without the perplexity and the disappointment that love was not more than this, when love's virtue lies not in being more than it is, but in being the pleasure of not being precisely this.

Again he raised his eyes to the veranda facing him. The children were not there, and the man, bent over his bowl, was eating his soup. That mystery of the Incarnation, the friar had

spoken very well today, explaining his meaning eloquently. But
the meaning of the Incarnation he did not need to have explained to him. One who had loved with body and mind as he
had, who had written of Love as he had written, and who had
never liked children, as he had not, possessed an experience of
the Incarnation that the friar did not have. Precisely because
everything had incarnated in him without being incarnate, and
had devoured his very flesh, leaving him that foul rag that he
now was, who better than he knew what the Incarnation was?
Or, at least, as well as a man could know it? To feel pregnant
with a poem, to feel onself made fertile by a glimpse of lightning, and to be a man—this was as much as one could know. It
is not known by the woman who gives birth, for it is their lot to
give birth, at times without having loved. It is not known by
the man who wants to have sons, for he can make them without
love. But the poet who has practiced love even at the cost of his
own flesh, who has written poems even though the spirit thinks
poetry a small thing, this one, yes, this one knows what manner
of thing is the Incarnation. But he merely knows it. He has not
lived the Incarnation, it is the Incarnation that has lived him.
And it is this that is the great mystery, not the other. And this is
the great difference between a god who is incarnated, and the
man in whom the Incarnation is played out. A difference that is
in the end a comedy, or can be seen as a comedy, for every man to
whom this happens is Amphitryon, a husband betrayed by the
Jupiter within him.

Before him he continued to see the illuminated stage, and
the figures declaiming verses. The door creaked and small light
steps sounded behind him. The thin, sharp voice began its
toneless recitation.

"Padre Manuel was here today, looking for you, and I told
him this was the day you go to St. Dominic's, and he told me he
had forgotten, and I asked him when he would return, and he
answered that he needed to ask you about your book, but there

was no rush, he would come back another day, or you should go seek him tomorrow or thereafter. What does he have to do with your book, always asking you things? Does a book like this, which is not of Our Lord God and of our holy religion, need you constantly to explain what this is, what that is, and to tell your life story, even if it is to your evangelist? May the Most Holy Virgin pardon me, but it seems to me a great sin. To tell your life to other people is a great sin of vanity. One's life should be told to the father confessor, and we must perform the penances that he orders for our evil words and deeds, and that's all. Then, in the hour of our death, we tell whatever we still remember or have done meanwhile, and the priest gives absolution, if we were virtuous and pious and never faltered in our duties to God and to His Church. Ah, Senhor Rui Dias's servant also came, sent by his master who is your great friend, to ask after the commission he gave you for those poems of King David, may God keep him. And I said that you had not yet finished but would soon do so, and that you've worked much and have even studied much with Padre Manuel so that the holy words would come out right and in their proper places. And he said that his master is greatly vexed with you, for it has been more than many months since he commissioned them, and you were doing nothing, and that he had already paid in advance for part of the work. And I said it was true, that he had already paid, but that in these matters paying something in advance is like giving cloth to the tailor, for the tailor cannot make a doublet without the cloth, and you cannot write without eating. And I told him that your pension was late and had not been paid, and that I had great hopes in the goodness of his master and in the great power he holds at Court so that the pension might be paid on time, for well you deserved it from His Highness for the many services rendered by your father, God rest his soul, and also for your services, for you used to be a foolish boy, and you were unlucky in life, also you were a man who wrote books and knew much of human and divine things, as Padre Manuel told me, and as Frei Bartholomew wrote in the endorsement he gave you. . . ."

"Frei Bartholomew said only that I knew much of human things."

"Exactly. Because knowledge of divine things you could have gained if you had studied seriously and been prudent, and you could even be a bishop today, much more likely than those two. But you had to involve yourself with bad women and bad company, and today you are what you are, and instead of it's being you who gives out endorsements, you have to ask them of others. If they weren't your friends and if you hadn't worn out their patience and demonstrated that you are a man repentant of the bad life he's led, they wouldn't give it to you, for these friars, may Our Lady pardon me if someone hears me. Your father used to laugh at them and say that they were all loafers, that they wanted only to eat and to have other men's women. God forbid, and that's why God punished him with that miserable death, without even a Christian burial. But you might go seek out the Duke, or Senhor Dom Manuel, and remind them that your pension is late, and there's nothing they cannot do, such powerful lords they are, cousins of the king. I had to go out to visit your godmother Joaquina who is having her pains once again and has no one to care for her, but I told her right away that I couldn't stay long, for today was your day to go to St. Dominic's to purify your soul, which you well need, and that you were coming back soon, hungry and wanting your supper, and that you'd get annoyed if I wasn't home to give you your soup when you arrived—and she answered that you were no child crying for his mother's breast, and it's true too because I used to put you to my breast as soon as you opened your mouth to scream. But that you never cried for the breast is true, you only used to cry afterwards because my milk was weak and we had to bring in a wet nurse, and your father wanted you to be nursed by a wet nurse because it wasn't befitting our condition that you be nursed at the breast of a lady such as I, wife of a man such as he, all people of substance. But the only substance we had was what he earned, and God knows how I lived after your father was gone and you were wandering in those lands of heathens and infidels for so long, and I never knew if you were dead or alive. I had news only when the armadas would arrive and some acquaintance came to tell me about you. And he would tell me that you had gone to this and that place, or that you were who knows where, since to me all those Indies are the same, and the names of the lands belong to the devil himself, God forgive me, only apostates can understand them. Many a time I thought you would write to me, but you never wrote, and many people told me that there you would write letters for others, for you always knew how to write well, ever since you were little, but you put lovely things on paper for them, and nothing for me. And I went on praying to Saint Anne and to Our Lady and sometimes I'd even change saints so that none of them would grow weary of hearing me, always fearful that you had died in the wars and the shipwrecks, or of those illnesses they have there, and I thought at times I could be praying for your good fortune and the prayers might in the end serve to reduce your days in Purgatory for your sins and frivolities, and the body to which I gave birth might be being eaten by the fish or the heathens, without Christian burial, like your poor father, may God keep him, and I only learned of it long afterwards. And your godmother Joaquina gave me this pie I've brought, which is made of a chicken her neighbor gave her, or half a chicken only, from which she made this pie, and she told me she had another and that she sent you this one, but she wanted you to write a prayer in verse to Saint Crispin, whose devotee she is, and I said that you would certainly write it after eating the pie."

"The pie I'll eat, but write verses to the saints I won't."

"Dear God, if someone should hear you and think that you don't believe in the saints. The Holy Inquisition which delivered us from the evil and malice of the enemies of our Faith orders us to believe in the saints, and yet I know that you don't believe, that you ask nothing of them, and it's from the sin of pride, according to what Padre Manuel told me when I spoke to him of my anguish at your not believing in the saints, and he answered me that you find the saints too small for you and that you're satisfied only with Our Lord God. I even shuddered at the thought of the danger we run in not having a saint to protect us. If it wasn't for the Duke and Senhor Dom Manuel and Senhor Rui Dias and other such lords, I'd like to see on what you'd live, for the king would never have heard of your existence. May God forgive me, but it's not God who's never heard of you, for he knows us all and is such a loving father that he never takes his eyes from us. But there he is, in his divine majesty, busy ruling the World, and no one ever won a cause without an advocate. Saint Anne has never failed me, and I don't even know what would become of me and you without her. Even this pie is a miracle of hers. When I went out to visit godmother Joaquina, I was saying to myself that Saint Anne would manage things so I wouldn't return home empty-handed but would bring some morsel for my son, and I even asked for a chicken pie, which seemed the most likely because godmother Joaquina always has chicken pies. I didn't promise Saint Anne that you would do what Joaquina wanted, because I know you and there's no counting on you for anything more than eating the pie. And that's why it won't do any harm if you don't write the verses to Saint Crispin, because it was no promise of mine. Your godmother's the one who said that you, if you wished, could do it, for everyone was saying you have a way with words, and that you could quickly write whatever verses were asked of you. And I answered that that must have been before, because now you had a very good commission, of great revenue, from Senhor Rui Dias, who does us the honor of being your friend, to put into verse the psalms of King David, may God keep him, and that you weren't writing anything, and this very day his servant was here complaining because of the payment that was advanced. Are you sleeping, aren't you listening to what I say? Eat your soup while it's hot and then this pie which must be delicious if it's like the last one godmother Joaquina made. I already had my supper at her house, and, besides, I lose my appetite just from seeing you in this state, such a strong and handsome boy as you were, all the girls used to turn around to look at you and all the men would bite their tongues with envy. And when the sun shone on your hair, I used to say to myself that my son was like a king with a crown on his head, or, God forgive me, like a great saint resplendent in gold on a procession day. And I used to stay and watch you go down the street, so vain that you never even looked back, with your hand on the hilt of your sword, and your steps so firm, my God, that it seemed that the earth was all yours. For this and other reasons your misfortunes began, with the brawls and the fights, and the evil deed, the worst misfortune of them all, of stabbing that man on Corpus Christi day, that shameless scoundrel who ruined you and made you leave for India and who deserved to die in sin, may God forgive me if it's I who sin. It's gotten so dark that I'll light the lamp. But the flame has gone out and I have to go downstairs to the neighbor and ask her for some fire. May our Lord God have pity on me, old and tired and with a grown son, yet I'm the one who has to go down the stairs to get the fire, for there is none in my house."

He opened his eyes to the shadows and the silence. He knew the corners of the room so well that it was as if he were seeing the chest and the oratory with the little branch wedged in, the small paintings of saints hanging, the shelf with the plates leaning against the wall, the cot in one corner, where he slept, the door to his mother's alcove and the door to the kitchen. He saw it all with the same certainty and detail with which he had seen Vasco da Gama's ships sailing in the sea, and there below, scenes of the Empyrean; with which he had seen

Venus embracing Jupiter and crying; with which he had
seen Adamastor emerge from a thick cloud; with which he
had seen Veloso running down the mountain. But he had
stabbed Borges, why? So that his life might change its course, so
that it would take its fated course, so that the Indies would be
imposed on him by his star, so that his star would come into
existence. My errors, ill fortune, fiery love, together have conspired for my perdition, there was no need of errors or of fortune, love alone for me would have been sufficient. Perdition.
Love alone. How false poetry is, and how true. How it speaks,
not speaking, and it is in not speaking that it speaks. How we
know nothing of our soul before writing it down, and how it is
not our soul that we know after having written. Perdition seeks
itself like a man who undresses to bathe in the sea, resembling
Leander crossing the Hellespont. And love alone would be
enough, like the moment in which all is forgotten, all disap-
pears, all evaporates, in the heat that blazes and lasts only an
instant, but an instant in which time is suspended, is petrified
in a space and a form, and all true space flees swiftly, running
through time until it itself becomes the time that was suspended. Merely this, because it is an image of supreme love,
beyond that terrible pool. Beyond or beneath? And if this love
were no more than an image, an ultimate essence of his own life?

Mysteriously, in the silence and the flux of his thoughts,
the pool opened, rare and translucent in its black depth, with
the tiny forms floating, and one was rising, rising, taking on the
color and features of a terrifying medusa. But the door creaked,
and a vague brightness made the objects emerge as flat forms,
shadowless in the weak light. The small light steps sounded.

"The neighbor says that in the interval before you arrived,
when I had already gone out, there also came that man who
asked you for poems for that gentleman who doesn't have a
Christian name, Senhor Dom Leonis. Everybody came here
today, it's like the Judgment Day. And he's going on a voyage

and was therefore very sorry not to see you, and he said to her that he left you many greetings and that he very much hoped your health would improve, and she answered that you really were very worn out, and he said that you would never wear out, because you were a great poet, one of the greatest that had ever existed in the world, something like, I'm not even sure who he said. And she laughed much and told him that Padre Manuel also said the same thing and that it was just their kindness, because this business of poetry never brought anyone anything. Just that in your case they gave you the pension, but it was because of the printed book and the many services to the king that your father performed in his poor life, and you too. And he answered that things always happened that way, that glory only came too late and that rewards, when they were given, never came according to what people truly deserved. I think that's to deny the infinite goodness of our Lord God, and it's not very respectful toward His Highness who gave you the pension. What you have to do is to go to Court to complain about their not paying you on the very hour and day, for I'm tired of dragging myself there, and they always ask me why you don't go, and the other day the treasurer even told me that it was all make-believe, that you didn't go because you had died, and that if I wanted to receive it I had to ask the king for a pension in my name. And you don't go because you have this sin of pride, and you don't want them to see you on crutches asking that they pay you what they owe you. I'm truly tired, and I'm going to lie down for I can't take any more. Be careful with the lamp, don't waste too much oil, for it costs an arm and a leg, and you know I'm afraid of fires and you might fall asleep there at the table, it wouldn't be the first time, and the lamp could set fire to your papers, to the house, may God help us and Saint Barbara protect us. If Senhor Rui Dias's servant returns, what shall I tell him? You don't even answer, you're almost dropping with sleep right on the table. Be careful with the lamp. . . ."

He sat watching the delicate sparks that the lamp gave out, like an aureole around a burning center. If Rui Dias's servant, or he himself, were to appear, he would say that in other times he was a youth, content and in love, beloved and esteemed, filled with the many favors and graces of friends and ladies, which heightened his poetic fervor, and that now he had neither the spirit nor the contentment for anything. . . . It would be 365 lines, as many as the days of the year, like a via sacra of life, 73 stanzas of 5 lines each. . . .

He rose, impelled by a yearning that took his breath away, a dizziness that multiplied in the tiny light of the lamp. Leaning on the table, he dragged himself to the far side and from there let himself fall to the cot. Rummaging in it, he drew out of one corner some sheets of paper, the small inkstand with the quill stuck through the ring, which, ever since his first voyage, he had been accustomed to keep thus. On his knees, with the pains there and in his parts increasing sharply in stings that made him grit his teeth, he moved to the table, placed on it what he was carrying, and raised himself. For one moment he stood, eyes closed, panting. Already the words rioted within him, confused with those others, useless and dead, from the translation he had attempted. They were like a tremor running through him, in shivers and light hesitations, concentrated in small patches of his skin. Bending over the table on which he was leaning, he pulled the chair to his side and fell into it, seated. A cold sweat ran down his forehead, and, as he opened the inkstand, he saw that the backs of his hands shone like pearls. A wave of joy flooded over him, in anguished jolts. His eyes burned and it was with tears. Everything had failed, everything, and poetry itself had abandoned him, fearful of his penetrating soulful eyes that saw into the depths of things. The pool with its floating forms. But he was a great poet, he transformed into poetry whatever he touched, even misery, even bitterness, even poetry's abandonment. All atremble but with a firm hand, he began to write. . . . By the rivers that flow from Babylon to Zion I found myself seated. . . . He scratched it out, desperate. And began again. By the rivers that run past Babylon I found myself and there sat weeping for memory of Zion and all that befell me. . . .

And he wrote on into the night.

1964                                    *Translated by Daphne Patai*